ROMAN'S GOLD

SHIFTER PARANORMAL ROMANCE

ANN GIMPEL

Edited by
ANGELA KELLY
Illustrated by
FIONA JAYDE

CONTENTS

ROMAN'S GOLD

UNDERGROUND HEAT, BOOK ONE

By
Ann Gimpel

Shifters keep their friends close and their enemies closer in a shadowy world where the line between hunter and hunted thins, blurs, and finally shatters

COPYRIGHT PAGE

BOOK DESCRIPTION, ROMAN'S GOLD

Once respected members of society, shifters are running for their lives. In a futuristic world where resources are scarce, Kate uses her human form to work as a sex surrogate. Furious at what looks a lot like genocide for her people, she joins the shifter underground.

Devon's been a cop for a long time. He has shifter blood, but not enough to change into anything, at least not until the police department insists on a series of infusions to make him better at tracking shifters so they can be imprisoned—or killed.

Devon's latest assignment is Kate. From the moment he sees her, he can't get her out of his mind. But she's the enemy he's sworn to eradicate. As he tracks her, the line between hunter and hunted explodes.

Against reason and wisdom, Kate and Devon defy the rules. If their passion doesn't save them, it'll doom them forever.

The story of the Underground Shifter Movement is fantastic. As more and more shifters are imprisoned and their rights are stripped away for being "non-human" the shifters have decided to unite and try to fight back. This goal is constantly hovering in the background driving the story forward with the romance helping it all along the way.

There was some excellent world building, but I am looking forward to more world building as well. The writing style is great. She has a way to flow words that just seamlessly come together to suck you into the story. I can't wait to see what is going to come now. A Sexy, Steamy, Shifter filled 5 PAWS!

CHAPTER 1

Kate Roman sauntered down Telegraph Avenue, the sounds of the constant Berkeley traffic loud in her ears. The city had banned hovercraft when air quality got so bad people needed masks to venture outside. The air still made the back of her throat burn, but at least her eyes didn't tear up.

She pushed her dark glasses up her nose and wrapped a colorful scarf more tightly around her hair. Someone was following her. She'd caught a whiff of something unusual with her feline senses half a dozen blocks back. Her perceptions weren't as sharp in her human form, but they gave her a definite edge. Who was back there? Try as she might, she couldn't identify their scent. She didn't want to stop and turn around. So long as her pursuer thought himself invisible, he—or she, or it—wouldn't do anything rash.

She hoped.

Her heart beat a little faster. No cause for alarm. Not yet, anyway. She worked as a sex surrogate, and there had been hundreds of clients over the past several years. Her hair was unmistakable with its bright red tone and warm, golden streaks. Clients sometimes trailed after her. Too shy to approach directly, yet drawn to her because of the best—sometimes the only—sex they'd had in their lives, they just liked to be close. Even though they had no idea she was a shifter, it played into the equation too. Humans were attracted to her animal energy.

Shy clients were one thing. The other options were scarier. Humans had made a big push to get rid of shifters. Because killing them outright would've engendered a great hue and cry from personal rights groups, they'd been imprisoned in droves. Conditions were so deplorable, many of her kin had died. Others were desperately ill. Apparently the personal rights groups weren't into visiting prisons to check on things. Disgust twisted Kate's features into an annoyed scowl.

Appalled by what was looking a lot like the beginning of genocide, she'd joined the shifter underground, a group masterminding escapes for those like her. Of course, the escapes were only the first step. Once out, shifters almost always needed medical care. They had to be hidden until their magic recovered enough to shield themselves. Many opted for dramatic plastic surgery to obliterate any trace of who they'd been when captured.

Kate blew out a tense breath. She had three post-surgical shifters concealed in the basement of her home in the Berkeley Hills. A coyote, a mountain lion—like her—and a bear were sequestered behind a hidden wall panel. She hadn't expected them to stay quite so long, and her pantry was almost bare. She glanced at her wrist computer and clicked a few keys. Ration Coupons flashed on the screen, followed by the numerals one and zero.

Shit.

Even if the food was only for her, ten coupons wouldn't buy much more than a day's worth, and her account wouldn't be replenished for another four days at the beginning of the next month. No way around it. She needed to put in an emergency call to the underground, once she got to her office where no one could hear. They had code words for everything, but still…

Kate tilted her head back. Her nose twitched. Whoever was behind her was closer. Not much, but a little. Should she turn around? She glanced at the cross street. Another half block and she'd be at her office. Someone jostled her shoulder. She pulled back, wary of a trap. Kate strengthened the illusion that softened her lengthened incisors and muted the sharp angle of her cheekbones and jaw.

"Sorry," a man muttered and pushed past.

She stared after him and reached out with a dribble of shifter magic, exhaling sharply.

Just a human. Damn! Definitely not who'd been following her.

Garden-variety cops had genetically-altered enhanced abilities. They smelled different. Trackers, elite police squads targeting shifters, had their own unique scent. She pressed her tongue against her teeth, thinking. What she smelled behind her was different from either of those. Did that mean it wasn't a cop—or a Tracker?

Not necessarily. He could be using one of their tricks to mask his spoor. Her throat tightened. She tried to swallow, but her mouth was too dry.

Enough excitement for one morning.

Kate lengthened her stride, loped across the street, taking advantage of an amber light, and took the steps to her office in a renovated Victorian two at a time. She ran her palm over the keypad. The electronics hummed, and the door clicked open. Safely inside, she shut the door and reset the lock.

Annoyance tinged with fear made her stomach roil. Against her better judgment, she turned and peered through a frosted glass side panel next to the thick, carved oak door. Eyes narrowed, she used her feline vision to take a good, hard look at who was walking down the sidewalk. After a couple minutes of nothing, she chided herself for being paranoid.

Kate was about to turn away and get ready for her first client when a man caught her attention. Boy, did he catch her attention.

He was tall, maybe six feet four, with broad shoulders and slender hips. Form-fitting jeans, a knitted dark blue top, and a brown leather vest showcased his body as if they'd been made just for him. Well-muscled arms and thighs rippled beneath his snug clothing. Maybe because of her work as a surrogate, Kate focused her gaze on his crotch.

Wow.

If he looked like that soft, he'd have a hell of an erection. Waist-length black hair swirled around him. Dark eyes, set in Native American bone structure, stared right at her building, almost as if he sensed her looking at him.

What was he? Human, but not. Unfortunately, she couldn't identify much. Wood and glass absorbed most of her magic. Kate moved away from the window. Heat poured through her. Her nipples pebbled into hard points. Whoever was out there was the most sexually-charged man she'd ever come across. Was he the one who'd been following her?

She snorted. Part of her hoped he'd been tracking her—she itched to jump his bones. In spite of being aroused, she felt edgy. He could be a member of the elite Tracker hit squads targeting shifters. Her underground organization had received intel the enemy was using more sophisticated strategies to trap them.

If they start using sex, we're done for.

Her lips curled into a wry grin. Shifters loved sex. It was a weakness from their animal sides.

"No, it's a strength," the mountain cat who lived inside her commented smugly.

"Hold on, sweetie. You'll get your fix soon enough."

"I don't want human sex," her cat complained. *"Find a shifter for us."*

"Enough of this. I have to get ready for my first client."

Her cat grumbled.

Kate smiled indulgently. She'd dreamed her bond animal like all shifters did when they hit puberty. The animal had picked her, but she'd sealed the deal by accepting it. The cat was a part of her, but its own entity as well. That included having opinions that sometimes diverged from hers.

She consulted her wrist computer. Not much time to spare. Kate walked through her spacious office. Furnished with late nineteenth century antiques to match the building's architecture, it was a homey place with overstuffed floral couches and chairs and golden oak tables. A small computer desk allowed clients to enter their personal data—or as much of it as they were comfortable divulging. Unlike the world's oldest profession, men actually needed a doctor's referral to see her. Kate liked it that way. She'd never had problems with any of her clients. The doctors screened them for diseases before sending them, which was another plus, though not exactly necessary. Virtually all the men who came through her door were virgins, and she was immune to human ailments.

A lush bedroom with a four-poster bed and an inventive assortment of toys sat behind the front office. Off to one side was a marble-inlaid bathroom featuring a sunken tub big enough for two, with Jacuzzi jets. Mirrors lined the walls. The gleaming gold fixtures and green-veined marble glowed invitingly. Water was good for loosening up nervous clients. Her first task was getting them used to being naked.

She ducked into her private quarters—a small room off the bedroom—dropped her bag in a corner, and stripped off her street clothes and shoes. Pants were a no-no in her business. She needed skirts with nothing under them, in case a client got hard, and she needed to move fast. Most of the men who visited her had erectile issues. Either they came too fast, or they couldn't get hard at all.

She pulled a teal jersey top out of a drawer and tugged it over her head. The soft folds of the fabric molded to her body. No bra. Looking at the curves of her breasts was good for clients. She traced the outline of a nipple through the silky fabric. It stiffened instantly. A vision of the man in the street slammed against her, and her nether regions flooded.

Kate grinned. She felt sorry for her first client. She'd probably attack him before he even got his clothes off.

She stepped into a black skirt with an elastic waist and grabbed a hairbrush. Red-gold curls cascaded nearly to her waist. A smattering of shiny lip gloss and she walked into the bathroom to check her appearance. Perfect. She looked about twenty-five. Good for when she needed to play the innocent in seduction charades. She blew a kiss at the glass. Not bad for a three-hundred-year-old shifter.

Three hundred six, her inner voice corrected. Kate laughed. She wasn't exactly immortal, but she'd live for hundreds more years before her face betrayed any sign of age.

The front bell chimed. Hector was right on time. Bare feet pattering over the thick, Oriental carpet in her front office, Kate strode to the door and peered through the safety viewer. She rolled her eyes. He'd brought flowers. She waved her palm over the electronically controlled lock, and the latch clicked open.

"Hi, gorgeous." Hector stepped inside and waited for her to lock up before handing her a bouquet of expensive-looking hothouse blossoms. She laid them on a side table. They'd keep for an hour out of water.

"Why, thank you. They're lovely. Hi there yourself, handsome." Kate smiled at him. She liked Hector. At forty-five, he'd decided it was time to find a wife. Problem was, he'd spent his entire life locked behind a computer screen and had no idea how to even say good morning to a woman, let alone ask for a date. All his sexual experiences had been with his hand until he tried to hire a hooker and failed miserably. He'd come while she was unzipping his pants and hadn't been able to get hard again.

He shook light brown hair back from a high brow. His hazel eyes shone with pleasure. He wasn't bad looking, but he needed to get outside. His skin was pasty white and his body soft. She'd suggested he join a gym and walk at least half an hour out-of-doors every day. She wondered if he'd taken her up on either suggestion.

His hand snaked out and curved around one of her breasts. She glanced between his legs, pleased to see the swell of an erection. Good. He wouldn't make her work very hard today. Kate cocked her head to one side and pressed her breast into his hand. "Business first. That will be five hundred credits."

His eyes widened. "You're giving me a break today."

"Not really." She cupped his hard-on. "Looks like you won't need much from me."

Color stained his fair cheeks. "Funny thing. It got hard when I was on the bus. Just thinking about you…" His voice trailed off.

"That's the way it's supposed to work. Pay up, so we can get those clothes off you."

He went to the computer, bent over, brought up his account, and transferred money into hers. The printer whirred. She grabbed the piece of paper, tore off one end, signed it, and handed it to him.

He came around behind her, closed his hands over her breasts, and nibbled her neck. "Mmm, you always smell so good."

She leaned against him for a moment, then led him into the bedroom and closed the door. One of the best things about being a surrogate was she trained her clients to do exactly what she liked, while cautioning them that part of lovemaking was communication. What she liked might not work for a different woman.

She turned toward him. His shirt and sports coat lay on a chair and he'd stepped out of leather loafers. His fingers were busy with the fastenings of his slacks.

"Pretty good progress," she said, flashing him a warm smile. "First time you came here, it took me most of the session to get your shirt off."

He shrugged. His pants pooled around his ankles. He stepped out of them and shoved his boxers down his hips. Kate felt her eyes widen. He was more than ready. Not just hard, but a drop of semen glistened in the center of his glans.

"Do you want to undress me?" she asked.

He closed the distance between them, put his arms around her, and kissed her. She kissed him back, aware of her own arousal. Hector didn't have much to do with that. But he'd give her something to think about other than the wonderfully seductive stranger she'd seen through her window. She pressed her breasts against him and thrust her hips against his hard-on.

Hector broke their kiss. He slid his fingers under her top and tugged it gently over her head. His gaze locked on her breasts before he took them in his hands. He twirled her nipples just the way she'd shown him. He'd been surprised when she told him women could come just from that.

She curved a hand around his erection. It bucked in her hand. He hadn't had problems with premature ejaculation the last few visits, but he seemed more excited today. "Do you need to be inside me?"

His breath came fast. "Could I? All I've thought about is—" His cock jumped in her hand again. Fluid leaked from it. She rubbed it around the velvety top with a gentle fingertip.

Kate backed toward the bed. "How do you want me?"

His gaze sought hers. "Could you be on top? I've done like you said, you know, playing with myself and fantasizing."

"Sure." She waited for him to lie down. Kate got a condom out of the night table drawer, opened the wrapper, and rolled it onto him. She straddled him and lowered herself onto his shaft. He groaned. She took care to keep her hips still. "Tell me when it's okay to move. Open your eyes. Look at me. Think about breathing. You can control this."

The line of his jaw clenched, and then softened. He cupped her pussy in an outstretched hand. Tentative at first, he rubbed her clit when she pushed into his hand. Her muscles closed around his cock. He rubbed harder. She laid a hand over his to show him the rhythm she needed.

"Is it okay if I make you come this way?"

"More than okay." With her fingers atop his to guide him, he rubbed harder and faster over her sensitive tissue. She knew she was moving around his erection, but hoped he had enough to think about besides coming that he'd be able to control himself. "I'm going to take my hand away. Now you do the same thing."

"Like this."

"Um-hum." She felt a familiar tightness, tried to hold back so she could savor things, but it was too late. She came, shoving her pussy against his hand. A vision of the gorgeous man she'd seen in the street danced behind her closed lids.

Deep in her mind, the cat purred, *"Yesssss. Find that one for us."*

Kate shushed it.

Hector had learned well. He kept moving his fingers until her hips quieted. "Wow. That was amazing," he crowed. "I got to watch you come. Your nipples got really hard, and you're all rosy."

"And you didn't come yourself. Even better." She laughed. "Is it okay if I move now?"

"Will I be able to make you come again?" She heard a hint of masculine pride in the question.

"No question."

He held out his arms. "I want to feel your breasts against me."

She lowered her torso until it touched his. "Very good. Asking for what you want is important. Women aren't mind readers. Put your hands on my hips. Move me the way you want to be fucked."

"What about you?"

"I had a turn. Besides, you can always touch me or lick me."

"You haven't taught me about licking." His voice had a catch in it.

"Well, if we don't get there today, there's always next time."

He gripped her hips. She let him control the movement, pleased it took him several minutes to come. Once his cock was through spasming inside her, she moved off his body and went to get a warm, wet cloth from the bathroom. By the time she returned, he had the condom off. She held out her hand. "I'll take it. Here." She handed him the cloth, dropped the condom into a waste can, and slid into a robe.

A disappointed look washed across his face. "Is our time up?"

"I'm afraid so."

"How many more visits do I have?"

"Not sure. Just a minute, I'll look." Kate padded into the outer office and clicked a few keys on the desktop computer. She was also buying a little time. Clients frequently got too attached, which was why she never told them up front how many visits had been authorized. Sometimes, even if they had several more sessions, she'd hedge, call their MD, and cut them off.

The truth was, Hector didn't really need her anymore. Seven visits had cured both his impotence and his problems with premature ejaculation.

"Good thing you asked." She breezed back into the bedroom, smiling brightly. "We've run through your sessions." He looked so crestfallen, she went to the bed, sat on the edge, and took his hands in hers. "Hector. You got what you needed here. You can make love with anyone now. You don't need me anymore."

"But I thought—I mean, I hoped..." Color crept up his chest to his neck and face.

"Aw, honey. Everyone falls in love with me. It's natural. I'm the first woman you had sex with." She patted his hand. "I guarantee you I won't be the last. Try asking that cute brunette you told me about out for coffee."

"Can I come back if I get into problems?"

"Sure. I'll square it with your doctor."

"Really?" He smiled. Hector was decidedly handsome when he did that.

"Really." She touched a finger to his chin. "You're quite the hunk when you smile. Remember to do it more often."

He dressed quickly, and she ushered him out the door. "Thanks again for the flowers. And best of luck, not that you'll need any. You'll make some woman very happy."

She closed the door, locked it, and looked at the time. She needed to call the underground about groceries, change the bed, and take a shower. It would be tight, but she was pretty sure she could work everything in before Todd showed up in half an hour.

Kate glanced at the calendar in her wrist computer. Good. Only two clients today. Worries about her three houseguests ate at her. It was better when she was home. The shifters in her basement were vulnerable by themselves.

CHAPTER 2

*D*evon Heartshorn strode past the pale blue Victorian. He'd watched Kate Roman run up the steps and let herself inside. He was nearly certain she knew she was being followed, but she'd played it very cool. Even though he hadn't been able to see her once the door was shut, his genetically-enhanced senses told him she'd been just inside, watching him.

He surreptitiously rearranged himself. Just following Kate had been immensely arousing. He'd known she worked as a sex surrogate, but he hadn't counted on her sheer animal magnetism or the hot swing of her hips. She was maybe five feet eight with curves to spare. Full breasts pushed against the front of her denim jacket. He'd gotten a good look when she'd been at right angles to him running up her office steps. Tight jeans displayed a generous butt.

It wasn't just her lush figure and the bright hair peeking out from under her scarf that heated his blood. The way she walked practically screamed she owned the street. She had presence, an almost regal bearing. Though she hadn't turned around, he knew from pictures that her eyes were amber, shading to golden. Cat eyes. Just like the cat she was.

She was magnificent. He didn't think he'd be able to capture her.

It would be a crime to put something that perfect behind bars. He shook his head. Dark hair fell into his face. He pushed it aside and ducked into a coffee shop. Everything was self-serve. He held his wrist computer up to the auto teller, ordered ten credits worth of food, and scanned his personal ID. The auto teller obligingly gave him a code, which popped up on his screen. Devon marched down the aisle. When he saw something he wanted, he scanned the barcode on his display, a glass door opened, and he took his item.

Coffee and pastry in hand, he sat at a table and raked his fingers through his hair. He wasn't pleased about his current assignment, but he didn't see any way out of it. He'd moved from the Mojave Desert three months ago to take a job as a lieutenant with the City of Berkeley Police Department. He'd even gone through the series of infusions to alter his already-enhanced genetics, so he'd be more sensitive to shifters. The last one had been three days ago, and his arm still ached. Something in the IV fluid was a hell of an irritant. He was glad to be done with that part of things.

His jaw tightened. Law enforcement had changed dramatically since he'd finished his criminal justice degree at UCLA. Devon had planned to go to law school, but first he'd needed to figure out a way to pay for it. Half Paiute from his father's side, he'd applied to the Tribal Consortium for an educational loan. Because he wasn't a full blood, they'd turned him down, and he'd ended up signing on as an officer with the San Bernardino County Sheriff's office.

A failed marriage and an underwater mortgage deep-sixed his law school plans. Fifteen years later, he was still working as a police officer. It wasn't such a bad life—until the governmental directive to round up shifters was signed into law two years ago.

A familiar pain knifed through him. His mother had been half-shifter; mixed genetics had cost her life. He'd petitioned the parole board to free her, had promised to keep a close eye on her. His request was denied.

"If we do it for her," the head of the board told him, "well, son, we'd have to do it for everybody's mother. I'm sure you understand."

Devon hadn't understood, though. The push to rid the United States of shifters made no sense to him. There may have been a few that used their animal forms to harm humans, but human criminals harmed humans too. His mother wasn't a threat to anyone. Not then, not ever. Her health had never been good, and she'd died in prison from a lung ailment, probably pneumonia.

Devon had visited her regularly. Even prisoners had rights and couldn't be denied visitors unless they acted out badly. His mother was far too ill to do anything but lay on her thin prison mattress, coughing. She'd told him not to grieve for her, but he couldn't help it. She'd only been fifty-seven. At the funeral, his two sisters and father hadn't said two words to him. He was a living, breathing representation of the ruling class, the reason his mother wasn't with them anymore.

He looked at his half empty cup of coffee and barely touched pastry, and his stomach knotted. He didn't feel hungry anymore. He'd wanted to talk with his family after his mother's death. After all, it wasn't like he'd been the one to round her up and stick her in that women's prison in Chino.

But I didn't do anything to help her, either. Guilt shriveled his soul. He'd given up after the parole board turned him down the second time.

Devon winced. He'd done his share of trapping shifters and seeing them imprisoned. Once the governmental directive had come down removing their human rights, he'd taken his responsibilities as a sworn law enforcement officer seriously. It didn't matter how he felt. He was bound by oath to uphold the law.

What about protect? the same inner voice nagged. *Aren't I supposed to protect the innocent?*

His mother had been one of the sweetest, kindest women he'd ever known. And now she was dead. Because of her blood. His hands fisted by his sides. He shot to his feet, almost tipping the flimsy table over, and stormed out of the restaurant. Blinded by guilt and rage, he ran square into a couple coming in.

"Watch it, dude," the man growled.

"Sorry." Devon stumbled to the side.

Outside the café, he walked fast, but it wasn't enough to assuage his guilt, so he broke into a run to ease the pain in his guts. He ran until the city limit sign flashed past and kept on going. He was off duty. No one expected him anywhere. If he went back to the station, they'd just grill him about Kate, and he'd have to fill out a report. Maybe he'd tell them he hadn't been able to find her. That might buy her a few more days of freedom.

He drew up hard and bent over, hands on his knees, sucking air. He'd never reneged on his duty before. He couldn't believe he'd even considered such a thing. If his superiors found out, he'd never work in law enforcement again. He might even get tossed in jail.

Yeah, just like Mom. Maybe it's what I deserve...

Devon worked his long hair into a single braid to get it out of his face, and then took off at a fast jog. Maybe if he ran long enough, the remorse sluicing through him would ease. He'd read the official paperwork condemning shifters—all of it. It hadn't made a whole lot of sense. After all, he had shifter blood, just not enough to change into anything. The rules were quite clear, though. Fifty percent was the dividing line. No one bothered to hide their shifter background. It was right on their birth certificates, so hunting them had been easy. Too easy, at least until some shifter organization had taken to wiping databases. He'd asked to be reassigned after his mother's death, but his desk captain laughed and told him to grow a thicker hide.

Shunned by his fellow officers for being soft-hearted, shunned by his family for his mother's demise, Devon finally couldn't stand it anymore. He had to leave the Mojave Desert with its painful memories. It had taken a while to find another job, but the City of Berkeley finally offered him an out. They had a new hush-hush task force. He'd only found out he'd be tracking shifters after he'd accepted the job, moved, and been sworn in.

The slap of his shoes against asphalt boomed loud in his ears.

Sweat ran down his sides. Hovercraft whirred overhead. The sky was thick with them outside the city limits. His throat stung. It didn't take much to erode the already-marginal air quality. A craft flew too low. Devon was certain it was in violation of the hundred-foot minimum, but didn't radio in the infraction. Why should he? His jurisdiction ended at the city limit sign.

"Hey, handsome. What you running away from? Got an angry woman on your tail?"

He whipped around. A young Asian, probably Vietnamese from the look of her fair skin and high cheekbones, smiled. He came to a stop, momentarily confused, and then smacked the palm of his hand against his head. Of course. Hookers weren't allowed inside the city limits, but many women set up shop close enough to Berkeley's edge to lure clients. Maybe a diversion was just the thing he needed.

"Nope. Just running." He smiled back.

She sashayed over to him, hips swinging. Her sarong gave him a fair view of the tops of her high, firm breasts. "It's been pretty slow today. You're quite a cutie. I'd be willing to give you a deal."

He quirked a brow, heart still pounding from his run. "What kind of deal?"

"Depends what you want." She tugged the low neck of her dragon-patterned, red and black dress aside, offering him a quick peek at a brown nipple.

Devon looked hard at her face. She was young. Past eighteen, but not by much. Part of him felt sad. He wanted to ask why she'd ended up selling her body, but didn't. He already knew the answer. It was more money than she could make at almost any job.

Better me than the next stranger she flashes. At least I'll be kind—and generous. His cock twitched, still lost in Kate's allure.

"Well?" She glanced away. "If you don't want to, I'll go back inside."

He gestured toward a flashing neon sign a few doors down. "Should we get a motel?"

"If you want to. It would save me some laundry."

"Sure. What's your name?" He held out a hand.

She took it, her grip firm. "Huong."

"Vietnamese?"

She nodded. "Yes, how'd you—"

He traced an index finger along her cheek. "Bone structure. And your name. Do you need to lock up?"

"No. My sister's inside."

Yes, and likely her mother and father and a few assorted uncles, aunts, and grandparents. Huong was probably supporting all of them. He wondered if her sister turned tricks too. He opened his mouth to ask, and then shut it with a clack. None of his business.

"Come on." He linked an arm through hers. "Let's go."

They walked to the nearby motel. She faded off to one side, waiting, while Devon went into the office. Key in hand, he gestured to her to follow and unlocked the door of room seventeen. Though the motel was well past its prime, the room was clean.

He turned the deadbolt and dropped the night lock into its slot. "You asked what I wanted. Straight sex is fine. If it's all the same to you, I'd like to shower first. I'm sweaty from running." He kicked off his shoes.

"Would you like me to join you?" The corners of her eyes crinkled when she grinned. She tossed a small shoulder bag next to the freestanding computer screen. It had hookups—hard and wireless—to accommodate all types of processers.

"Sure."

"I won't charge any extra." She drew the window curtain closed, turned on a lamp, then came to his side and tugged his vest off. She unbuttoned his shirt and reached around to unhook the clasp of the leather pouch he wore at his waist. He grabbed it from her and laid it on a table.

Huong shot a sad look his way. "I don't steal from my johns."

"Didn't think you did." He took a deep breath. "Look, you probably should know I'm a cop—"

She gasped and spun away from him, grabbed her purse, and headed for the door.

"Huong. I'm off-duty. I'm not here to bust you. I just thought I should tell you. You'll see the tattoos once you get my clothes off."

She stopped, one hand on the night latch chain. "Please don't arrest me. My family…" Her voice broke.

"You don't have to leave. I promise I won't arrest you. For one thing, my jurisdiction ended at the city limits. For another, prostitution is legal here."

She turned slowly and faced him, but made no move to sit. "That's not what the last city cop said."

He waited, but she didn't elaborate. His jaw tensed with anger. He was pretty sure he knew what one of his fellow officers had done. "I'm betting he told you that you had to service him or he'd arrest you."

Long hair fell over her face as she nodded.

"Well, if that ever happens again, you can tell him to go fuck himself."

She giggled, tossed her hair back, and looked at him. "You know something, cop, I like you."

"Good. Want to keep undressing me?" He winked.

Fingers busy again, she murmured, "It's a hundred fifty credits for an hour. I'll give you two for that."

"Do you have a way to transfer credits?" He'd always assumed hookers dealt strictly in cash, all of which was black market. The government had outlawed anything but credits about the time they forced shifters underground. They'd done a piss poor job of collecting all the cash, so it was still mostly all in circulation. Black market cash to purchase black market goods and services.

"Sure." She pulled his shirt out of his jeans and pushed it up his chest. She leaned close and licked his nipple. An electric shock radiated through his belly to his groin. "Hey, cop. You need to pull your shirt off. I'm not tall enough."

He whipped his shirt over his head and dropped it on a chair.

Huong whistled, and then ran her hands down his chest. "Nice muscles," she breathed, fingering the tattoos on his upper torso. "This is the cop one. What's this?"

"It's from my tribe. I'm half Paiute. The stag is my family symbol."

She arched a brow. "Indian. Interesting."

"How so?"

She grinned. "Means you're a brown-skinned foreigner just like me."

He laughed. "I suppose that's one way to look at it. Just remember, my people were here before any of the rest of you." He started unbuttoning his jeans. She shoved his hands aside and pushed the well-worn fabric down his legs with practiced ease. He stepped out of his pants.

"No underwear?" She ran her tongue over her full lips. "Sure you weren't cruising for a woman?"

"Never wear any." He considered explaining about Native traditions, but decided not to. Men from his tribe who lived on the reservation avoided things they considered white man's inventions.

"I can see why. Probably don't fit so well over this." She reached for his cock, already half-erect, but he shook his head.

"Shower first."

She untied a knot at her shoulder; her sarong slid to the floor. His eyes widened. She was lovely. Her breasts, tipped by brown nipples, rode high on her ribcage. A flat stomach, flared hips, and a smooth, shaven pussy nestled between long, shapely legs took his breath away.

His cock sprang to life. It had been months since he'd hired a woman to satisfy him. Devon wanted to toss her onto the bed, spread her legs, and plunge inside. Instead, he strode to the bathroom and flipped the taps. He felt the heat of her body right behind him.

Needle jets from a shower obviously sporting a low-flow showerhead pummeled his body. She pumped the wall-mounted soap holder a few times, rubbed her hands together, and lathered his body, lingering over his erection.

His heart thudded against his chest. He sucked in steamy air and backed her against one of the plastic-paneled walls. Her arms went around him, and she tilted her face upward. He kissed her. She opened her mouth to him, and her tongue sparred with his. Either she was a consummate actress, or she wanted him as badly as he wanted her. He felt her nipples harden where they pressed against him.

She broke away from the kiss. "Clean enough, cop?"

He realized he'd never told her his name, but there was no reason to. "Yeah, probably." Lust thickened his words. He turned off the jets. By the time he stepped out onto cracked linoleum, she was there with a towel. He didn't care about being dry. His cock curved along his belly, as hard as it ever got. He wouldn't last beyond a few strokes.

She knelt in front of him, but he pulled her upright. "I want to be inside you. Condoms?"

Huong scampered into the bedroom and pulled a foil packet from her bag. He grabbed it from her, ripped it open and rolled it over himself.

"Been a long time, huh?" She eyed him. One of her hands toyed with her nipples, the other dipped between her legs.

Devon couldn't talk. Her wantonness definitely turned up the heat factor. He tugged the faded bedspread off the bed. She understood and lay down, holding her arms out to him. He sank into them. It felt so good to have a woman close her arms around him. It didn't matter she was a hooker. For the next few minutes, he could pretend whatever he wanted.

He took her in his arms, pressed his body against her, and kissed her. Huong reached down to guide him home, and he sank his full length inside her. She brought her legs up and tightened them around his lower back.

He groaned at the feel of her, hot and tight around him. She thrust her hips upward. Her mouth opened wider under his. He tried to be still, but his cock had other ideas. It wanted to move, hard and fast, until it emptied inside the woman around it.

She tightened her hold on his back, nails digging in, and tore her mouth away from his. "Move, goddamn it," she urged, her voice raspy with passion. "You got me going the second I saw you run past my door."

He didn't need more of an invitation. He drew back until only the tip of him was within her and then slammed himself home, hard, fast, over and over. Her muscles clenched around him, and she cried out. If she was faking it, she was damned good. Devon stopped thinking. If he got any harder, he'd burst into a million pieces. Heat poured through him, electrifying his nerve endings.

A vision of Kate, naked with all that wonderful hair falling down her full breasts, danced behind his closed eyes. He was holding her, fucking her. She loved it. Loved him, couldn't get enough… Climax pounded through him. His cock jerked and came and jerked some more. He barely recognized the primal grunts filling the room as his.

He'd been supporting his upper body on his arms. They folded, and he collapsed atop her, panting.

Huong murmured wordlessly and stroked his back. "If I could have a man in my life, I'd want him to be just like you."

He grinned and pulled out of her, careful to keep hold of himself so the condom wouldn't leak. On his feet, he rolled it up his shaft and chucked it. "Bet you say that to all the boys."

"No." She gazed at him, her dark eyes serious. "I don't. It doesn't matter, though, cop. You have your life, and I have mine."

He reached for his discarded clothes and dressed. She was right. He had buddies who'd been dumb enough to fall in love with hookers. Occasionally, it worked. More often, jealousy tore the couple apart. He picked up his wrist computer. "Money?"

She unfolded her body from the bed, gathered her sarong, and tied it in place. "Code?" She pulled a wrist computer out of her small bag. "Hold on a sec. I'll get the voice recognition software up."

He punched a few buttons and rattled off the string of numbers that flashed across his display. It would authorize a credit transfer into her account. She tapped keys on her computer.

"All set." She smiled at him, but he thought he saw sadness behind it.

"Do you want me to walk you home?"

Huong shook her head. "No."

"Now that I know where you are, maybe we could—"

"You don't really mean that. Goodbye, cop. Thanks. It was fun."

Devon undid the deadbolt and night latch. He walked toward Berkeley and his small, almost unfurnished flat. Huong was right to tell him not to come back. Women had ways of knowing when the man between their legs imagined he was fucking someone else.

He settled into an easy lope. Kate filled his mind. He had to find a way to get close to her. By the time he ran up his steps an hour later, he had an idea.

CHAPTER 3

Kate cracked her door and swept the street with all her senses. She scented the air and blew out a sigh of relief. Whoever had been after her that morning hadn't stuck around. She didn't really expect they would. After all, it was a good five hours since she'd started her work day. She'd bundled Todd out the door half an hour ago. Another shower and change of sheets later, she'd dressed in street clothes and gathered her things. Normally, she would've sprinted out the door, anxious to get moving, but given this morning it paid to be cautious.

She checked the time and frowned. Only twenty minutes before she was supposed to meet the hovercraft with her groceries. She could've hunted to feed herself, but not all four of them. Her underground contact had chastised her for not bringing her car. Kate hated to drive in Berkeley traffic. Rush hour extended through practically the entire twenty-four hour time spectrum. She took the bus whenever she could.

Electronics whirred as the door locked behind her. Kate hurried down the steps and set off on the shortest route that would get her outside the city limits. The day was gray and cloudy. A fine mist dripped from everything. The pilot would be taking a risk picking her up outside an approved landing zone, never mind dropping her at her house, which was inside the city limits. Barely inside, but rules were rules.

She thought about the handsome man she'd seen in the street. Heat warmed her cheeks. She'd thought about him many times over the course of the day. She'd even pretended he was the one between her thighs when Todd—who'd finally managed a credible erection—was discovering what sex was all about. She grinned. The look on his face when he'd sunk full length inside her was priceless. He'd even managed to last a couple of minutes.

She hurried past the city limit sign. Berkeley was surrounded by dreary, concrete walls with gates. When civil unrest escalated, city cops secured the gates until things settled down. It worked because no one wanted to be locked inside their town. Suppliers complained too, when they couldn't deliver their goods. All in all, it had proven an effective means of crowd control.

She focused on her wrist computer, called the agreed upon number, and activated the app that would ping her location to the hovercraft. Kate scanned the skies. Hovercraft were nearly silent unless you were right next to them. They ran on electricity supplied by well-muffled onboard generators. In moments, the craft came into view over her head. A harness dropped from its belly. She buckled in and tried to relax as the auto winch brought her aboard. It wasn't easy. She was totally vulnerable to sniper pot shots as well as mechanical failures in the persnickety winch system.

Her head spun, and she realized she wasn't breathing. *Come on,* she urged herself. *It's not like I haven't done this before.*

Yeah well, I didn't like it then, either, another inner voice answered testily.

The upper part of her body was inside the craft. She placed a hand on either side of the opening and levered herself the rest of the way in. The door slid into its slot, and she undid the harness buckles with unsteady hands, dropping it over the winch.

"Stay down," the pilot called over a shoulder.

Kate looked longingly at the soft copilot's seat, then slithered against a curved wall and tried to get comfortable. "Are we good?"

"Yeah, I think so. No radio calls to land immediately and turn myself in." A short bark of a laugh followed the words.

"Sorry about the food crisis. I only thought they'd be with me for a week, but it's been nearly three."

The pilot blew out an audible breath. "Yeah, we're running out of hiding places. Not even sure you're all that safe anymore—"

"What?" She leaned forward, her heart beating harder.

"Uh, sorry. Thought your contact would've told you."

"He didn't tell me anything. As long as you opened your mouth, I need to know."

"Let me check what I can tell you."

The pilot keyed something into his console. A moment later, her contact—also the head of the shifter underground in California—shimmered into life on the screen. Max's mouth moved, but she couldn't hear him because the pilot had muted the sound. The screen faded to gray. "Okay," he said, "I was cleared to tell you some things."

Kate rolled her eyes. She'd taken a huge chance when she signed on to help the underground. It didn't sit well that they were keeping secrets from her. "Well?" she urged the pilot. "What did Max authorize you to tell me?"

"It's the new Tracker task force. They've gotten some sort of drug to make them more sensitive to us. According to Max, half a dozen of our hiding places were busted in the last week."

"I knew the first part—about the drug. Dear God. How many of us did they get?"

"Nearly a hundred."

She bit her lip. The next question was a hard one, but she wanted to know. "Have they started killing us yet?"

The pilot nodded. "Before they actually sign us into prison." He grunted in disgust. "Guess they figure if there's no official record, we never existed."

Kate dropped her head into her hands and rubbed her temples. "We have to fight back—before they kill all of us."

"We're talking about it."

"We're going to run out of time while we're talking." Her voice ended on a shrill note she didn't like at all. "Is it like this in the other cities too?"

Another nod. "Mostly even worse than here."

Kate sighed. "What's your plan for all that?" She gestured at the stacks of food crates surrounding her.

"I'll drop you in the woods behind your home. Scoped it out before I came to get you. It's actually outside the city. Not an approved zone, but I'll chance it. It will take less time to unload on the ground than it would if we used the winch to lower each box. A whole lot less."

She thought about the logistics of carrying the twenty or so boxes through thick woods to her house. It would take hours. "Can I get the other three to help? They're strong enough. In fact, two are well enough to leave—if there was anywhere for them to go."

"It would be best if they remained hidden. All you really need for tonight are a couple of boxes. You can bring the rest inside over the next few days."

"If no one finds them."

"There's always that," he agreed. "I'm starting down. Hang onto something since you're not strapped in."

"Earlier, you said I wasn't safe anymore."

His hands moved over the controls, and the hovercraft banked sharply. "It's that new task force. They may know who you are. We're not certain, though. Your best bet is to keep to your normal routine."

"Why? So they can find me."

"No, so you don't look suspicious."

"What if I don't agree with that strategy?" Her stomach clenched. The thought of capture and imprisonment made her want to jump out of her skin. Those like her didn't do well in prison. The guards passed them around just as freely as they did hookers. Apparently they hadn't heard about the part of the two-year-old law forbidding sexual congress with shifters.

The pilot ignored her question. "Landing in T minus ten, nine, eight…"

She gripped an aluminum strut and prepared for impact. Without wings or rotors, landings were jarring. The craft hit, bounced, and hit again. "Oomph." She groaned and rubbed her tailbone.

The whirr of the pilot's seatbelt as it retracted rang in her ears. He stood over her, hands extended. "Sorry about that. Let me help you up."

"Nah, I'm okay." She scrambled to her feet and draped the strap of her bag over one shoulder. "Let's get this stuff unloaded."

It didn't take all that long. The biggest time-guzzler was unshackling the boxes from where they'd been secured against the body of the hovercraft. She stood and watched the craft float into the air, then turned and looked at the stacks of crates. The woods were thick here. It was possible the food would stay hidden long enough to move it to her basement. She hefted a box. Not bad. If she was careful, she could stack them and take two at a time.

Kate turned in a circle. Everything looked the same.

Crap, which way is home?

Logic dictated downhill, but she wasn't certain. She sniffed, but all she smelled were trees and small rodents. She clicked the display of her wrist computer, activated a map program, and told it to find her address. It was sluggish because of the tree cover. Eventually, an arrow pointed to her left with the information beneath that she was eight tenths of a mile from her target location. She slid the computer into a pocket, picked up two boxes, and started walking.

She marked her route so she could find the boxes again. It was extra insurance. Her feline sense of smell would've been fine without physical symbols. Every time she stopped to notch a tree branch with her pocketknife or scratch something in the dirt, her skin crawled with apprehension, but it was nothing compared with her anxiety once she traded the forest canopy for open streets. It was only about a block to her house, but still...

Cat senses on high alert, shifter magic fanned about her, she crept forward. It would be impossible to explain why she'd emerged from the woods with two crates of black market food. If anyone so much as showed their head, she'd dump the boxes, shift, and make a run for it. She was fast as a mountain lion. Nothing human could catch her.

By the time she came around to her back door, Kate dripped sweat. The next nine trips would have to be after dark. She might have a heart attack if she had to run the gauntlet again in broad daylight. Kate pressed her palm to the lock, grateful for the modern electronics she'd installed a few years back. The door opened, and she shoved the boxes inside. Kate sank down on one of them, blowing hard. With shaking hands, she unwound her scarf and mopped her face with it.

Got to check on Tara, Joe, and Mike.

With their animal senses, they would've either heard or smelled her, probably both. They had to be hungry. There hadn't been any food since yesterday. She got to her feet and unlocked the door leading to the basement. Then she got one of the boxes and balanced it carefully while she made her way down the steep staircase.

Her house was over a hundred years old. Built around nineteen-twenty, it was made of wood and stone and glass. She'd blown into town with another new identity a few months before purchasing it. In those days, she'd worked as a schoolteacher. Normally, she'd have moved away long since, but most of the other houses around her had emptied out as the government made it progressively more difficult to own anything. She'd faked her death a few times and ginned up legal documents, leaving the house to a relative. A smattering of magic to alter her appearance with illusion and she was all set for another twenty-five years or so.

Kate left the lights out, feeling her way from the bottom of the staircase to the hidden wall panel. She used her feline night vision and punched in the code to open it. Joe grabbed the box out of her arms and dropped it on the floor. Mike pried it open with a claw. A bear in his animal form, he was partially shifted. Hunger was easier to tolerate that way.

"Wow, Kate. Thanks," Joe murmured, keeping his voice soft. He pulled a package of crackers and another of processed cheese out and ripped into them.

Kate glanced around. "Where's Tara?"

"Back here." The woman's soft voice sounded from a darkened recess. She was a coyote in her animal form.

"Come eat." Kate kept her voice neutral. She didn't want to tell them how bad things were out in the world.

The slightly built woman with long brown hair crept forward. Her eyes were swollen and her face blotchy. Kate wrapped her arms around her. "You've been crying. Are you feeling ill again?" Tara had been badly beaten in prison and sexually assaulted repeatedly.

Tara's dark eyes gleamed in the gloom of the basement. "No. I've been listening to the vid feed."

"What?" Kate drew back, put her hands on Tara's shoulders, and shook her. Not hard, but enough to get her attention. "You know that's against the rules. What if someone tracked a net use spike here? Everyone knows I'm gone at work all day. You'll give yourselves away."

"It's my fault." Mike set down a can of peaches and wiped the back of his paw/hand across his mouth. "We had to know what was going on. Being down here is almost as bad as being in prison."

"So one of you went upstairs and turned on my computer?"

"I did." Tara hung her head. "What I heard was so bad I ran away. The guys heard the door, came after me, and dragged me back."

"Where the fuck did you think you were going to go?" Anger raked Kate's nerve endings and made her stomach sour.

"We're putting you at risk." Joe stopped shoveling food into his mouth and looked at her. "It would be safer for you if we left." He shook tawny hair back from his face. A mountain lion like her, he shared her amber eyes and feline features.

The anger bled out of her. All of them were running scared. What they needed to do was stand and fight, except there weren't enough of them. Shifters were so long-lived, they produced very few children. They needed an edge and she had no idea what it might be. "There're a bunch more boxes of food in the woods," she said slowly. "You might hole up in some of the caves in the hills."

"I like that." Mike shimmered back to wholly human. Like all bear shifters, he had a burly build. Light brown curls fluffed around a strong-boned face. Hazel eyes glittered at the prospect of freedom. "It's not natural living in this basement. If the fuckers are going to kill me, I'd like to see the sky again and be a bear for a while." He made a grab for his clothes and got dressed.

"I second that," Joe muttered.

"Me, too," Tara chimed in.

"How about this?" Mike set his jaw in a determined line, and he laid a hand on Kate's arm. "Once it gets dark, you can show us where the food crates are. If you want, you could stay for a while. We could all shift and pretend it was like the old days."

"What a grand idea." Tara draped an arm around Joe and leaned into him. He hugged her back.

Kate shut her eyes and blew out a breath. "You may not be as safe—"

"From what I saw on the vid feed today," Tara interrupted, "you're not safe here. They've got this new elite task force. And a drug that makes it so they can smell us. I saw bunches of us being herded off to prison." Her voice caught.

Kate didn't bother to tell her about the shifters being shot.

"Anyway, we've decided," Joe said. "We were going to tell you once you got home. We really appreciate all you've done for us, but it's time for us to go."

~

AN HOUR AFTER FULL DARK, Kate crept from her house in human form. Her cat wanted out. It had been a struggle to keep it contained.

"But the night hours belong to cats," it whined. *"We never go out at night anymore."*

Kate tried to reason with her bond animal, but safety wasn't part of the cat's vocabulary. As far as she was concerned, curving canines, sharp claws, and speed could defeat any enemy.

Kate was dressed all in black, and she smeared dirt on her face to hide its pale tone. Once she got to the end of the street, she whistled, faded into the nearest trees at the edge of the woods, and waited. One by one, Tara, Joe, and Mike joined her. Kate led the way deeper into the woods, using her feline senses to track her earlier path from marker to marker.

"Here we are," she whispered. The others' hearing was just as acute as hers. She had no doubt they heard her.

"Kachingo! Jackpot!" Joe exclaimed and patted a box. Apparently he wasn't as worried as her about being overheard.

"This is great," Mike said. "Shit, wonder how the underground gets all this black market food."

Tara dropped her clothes on one of the boxes. In moments, she shimmered into a sleek coyote and took off at a run through the trees. The men followed suit. Joe nudged her with his muzzle. *"Join us?"*

She didn't think it wise, but the allure of her animal form was impossible to resist. Her cat screeched inside her head. *"Take your damned clothes off."* A reluctant smile curved Kate's lips. She loved her speed and her grace as a mountain lion. And the acuity of all her senses. Kate shucked her way out of her garments. She piled them atop the other clothes and gave her body the command to shift.

Yesssss...

Warm fur sprouted, her torso lengthened. Powerful

hindquarters bunched, and she launched herself after the others. Scents bombarded her. She could tap into her feline sense of smell as a human, but it was so much more acute after she first shifted that it was almost painful. Before the latest spate of governmental edicts a couple of years back, she'd taken to her animal form almost daily. Now she was lucky if she spent an hour a month as a mountain lion. Sometimes, she shifted in her house just to remember what it felt like. It wasn't enough to satisfy the cat, though, and it had gotten progressively harder to force it into submission. It growled and snapped and told her in no uncertain terms that shifters weren't meant to spend all their time in human form.

"You're free, sweetie. Go for it," she told the cat.

"I intend to."

Their muzzle twitched. Prey. A field mouse skittered a few feet ahead. Kate pounced. The wonderful taste of hot blood warmed her gullet. She crunched through small bones. Suddenly wary, Kate fanned magic around her. All she felt was Tara, Joe and Mike. After a moment's hesitation, she ran toward them. They were gamboling in a small clearing, and they looked so happy, goddamn it, that it broke her heart.

Just for tonight, I'll pretend right along with them...

A husky purr rippled from her throat.

Dawn was lightening the eastern skyline when she loped back to her clothes, shifted, and dressed. For once, her cat didn't complain. Kate trod the now familiar path toward home, taking care to undo her earlier markings with elbow grease and magic. No point in leading a poacher right to her friends. The underground weren't the only ones trafficking in black market food.

Kate unlocked her door. She figured it was around six. Fortunately, she didn't have clients until later in the afternoon. Though she didn't need as much sleep as humans, she was tired. Two or three hours of rest would help. She set the household alarm system, climbed the stairs to her bedroom, and sat on the edge of her antique four-poster bed to jimmy off her sneakers. She loved antiques, probably because she remembered when they'd been the newest fashion.

"We need a mate." The cat's comment came out of the blue.

Kate felt sad. It was a rare shifter lucky enough to find their mated partner. The one whose soul would link with theirs through the whole of their long lives. *"Great idea. Where do you propose we find one?"*

"I'll look. My instincts are better than yours."

"You do that, sweetie. Good hunting."

She thought about brushing her hair and her teeth, but opted for later and tugged a coverlet over herself. Just before sleep claimed her, the man's face from earlier rose from her memory. He was smiling right at her, dark eyes lit with sensual promise.

CHAPTER 4

Three days had passed since Devon's brief fling with Huong. He'd shuttled between work and home, but no matter where he was, Kate filled his mind. He couldn't get her out of his thoughts. Not that he tried very hard.

He'd hedged when his captain asked about his surveillance assignment. Keeping a poker face, Devon told the captain he thought their intel about Kate was incorrect because he hadn't been able to sense anything unusual about her. The captain cocked his head to one side and asked how long since Devon's last injection. His only comment before reassigning Devon to a different project was sometimes it took a while for the infusions to reach maximum potential.

During the intervening time, Devon had done mostly desk work and nonshifter-related surveillance. There'd been a rash of drug deaths, and he'd run down the ringleaders, who'd brought tainted heroin into the city.

The previous night he'd wakened from the most erotic dream he'd ever experienced, drenched in sweat and semen. He'd taken Kate from behind, holding the creamy globes of her ass tight against his cock as he pounded into her. Heart hammering, cock still throbbing, he'd turned on the bedside lamp, unable to believe he'd had a wet dream. That hadn't happened since he was fifteen. He closed his eyes. Her body, at least as he imagined it, was damn near perfect. And her hair was amazing. Long and thick, she'd wrapped it around his cock to tease him before he'd flipped her around and entered her.

The dream decided things. Mystified by his obsession with Kate, he had to do something to force a meeting. He'd already scheduled a doctor appointment to try to get a referral to see her as a surrogate, but it was still several days away. He couldn't chill that long. She was driving him crazy.

Maybe, if they were face-to-face, it would help him figure things out. Raw need frazzled his nerves. He couldn't wait any longer to sit next to her, talk with her, and inhale her intoxicating scent. It had been faint, but unmistakable, the day he'd trailed after her. Though he didn't understand how it was possible, her elusive aroma had dogged him ever since.

He didn't sleep much after waking from the dream. Mostly he'd tossed and turned and jacked off—again and again. Every time he thought he'd finally slaked his lust, Kate would bloom in his mind, and his cock hardened. By morning, he was tender and sore.

Unless the department called him in on a special assignment, no one cared whether he wore a uniform. Nerves thrumming with excitement, Devon tossed on jeans, a jersey, and his trademark leather vest. He parked several blocks from Kate's office and left his electronics in his cruiser.

He gazed at the front door of her office from behind a multilayered dumpster across the street. Despite being relieved of the assignment to shadow Kate, Devon had tracked her movements since following her in the street that day. He worked it in between his police duties, but that was easy enough to do. After three days, he had a good idea of her schedule. Soon, she'd head out for lunch in a small café a couple of blocks away. It was always crowded this time of day.

Maybe I can talk with her. Really talk with her...

Devon's throat tightened. His heart pounded faster than it needed to. A corner of his mouth turned down in a wry expression. He was acting like a love-struck kid, and he had no idea why. An erection pressed against the front of his jeans. He zipped his leather vest so it would do a better job of hiding his arousal.

Kate's door opened. She tripped down the steps as if she were in the best of moods, a broad smile parting her full lips. Red-gold hair floated around her. Some days it was in a bun or braided. Today, she wore it loose.

Devon balled his hands into fists. The bad thing about his surveillance point was he'd gotten to see her clients come and go. "Yeah, except they're mostly coming," he muttered. He wanted to be one of those clients. Needed to feel her arms and body wrapped around him. His balls tightened. For an awkward moment, he thought he might come where he stood.

He hastened from behind his hiding place and shadowed her down the street, keeping a respectable distance—and several people —between them. His dick settled, but not by much. Devon waited for a few minutes near the café before walking through its swinging door. He scanned the crowded room while he got himself a cup of coffee and a sandwich.

Once he got the lay of the land, he pressed his tongue against his teeth to keep from grinning like a fool. The only empty seat in the place was at Kate's small table. What an incredible stroke of luck. He pushed his way through groups of people standing in twos and threes. A dope deal was going down, but he ignored it. Nothing shy of one patron murdering another would make him switch to cop mode.

Maybe not even that. Depends how things go with Kate.

"Hi." He grinned down at her. "Mind if I join you?" He jerked his chin at the remainder of the room. "Sorry if it's an imposition, but looks like this is the last seat."

Her eyes widened. She opened her mouth and shut it again. Finally, she nodded curtly. "Sure. I won't be long."

"Don't rush off on my account. I could do with a spot of company." He squeezed his tall body into the plastic chair and set his coffee on the table. Devon unwrapped the plastic from his cheese sandwich and took a bite. It was stale and his mouth dry, not a good combination. He chewed for a while to get the gelatinous mass moving down his throat.

Kate looked away and spooned soup into her mouth faster.

"So—" he tried to look non-threatening "—do you live in the neighborhood?"

"No." The word held a bitten-off tone.

"Gee." He put his sandwich down and spread his hands in front of him. "Just trying to make conversation. I'm new here. Just moved to Berkeley a little while ago. It's really different here than in San Bernardino. People are more, uh, closed off." He shrugged and took a sip of coffee.

"Yeah, city folk can feel that way." Her gaze darted to his face, then returned to her food. "Because we live in such tight quarters, we learn to ignore people to preserve the illusion of privacy."

"Humph. You're pretty insightful. I hadn't looked at it in quite that way before."

"Thanks." She flashed half a smile. It made her amber eyes glow.

Devon felt a rush of raw sexual heat that nearly flattened him. Christ! All she'd done was smile, and she'd barely done that. His cock sprang to attention, so hard it was almost painful. He stifled a groan.

"Are you all right?"

He gulped his coffee. "Yeah. Fine." He inhaled raggedly. "Have you lived here for a long time?"

"A few years. My office isn't far from here. Um, what exactly do you do?" Her eyes shaded to gold and narrowed. She gazed at him intently.

Devon was ready for the question. He'd practiced what he'd tell her while waiting behind the dumpster. "I'm a short haul trucker. Work for a food processing plant just north of the city. By the way, I'm Devon." He held out a hand.

Kate pursed her lips. It was almost as if she knew he'd lied to her. "Kate." She touched his hand briefly. It sent a shock to the bottom of his belly. Her eyes flared in surprise, so maybe she felt it too.

Kate yanked her hand away. "So, um, Devon, have you always been a truck driver?"

"No. I graduated from college with a criminal justice degree. Wanted to be a lawyer once upon a time."

"What happened?"

He shrugged. "No money for law school." Devon flicked a finger against one of his high cheekbones. "I'm half Native American. Unfortunately, half wasn't enough for the tribe to underwrite my schooling. How about you?"

"I've been a lot of things. Taught school for a bit. Worked as a secretary."

The next logical question was, what do you do now? Devon girded himself and asked.

She lifted her chin defiantly. "I'm a surrogate."

He tried his best to look confused. "A what?"

"Sort of like a hooker, but my clients come from MDs." The corners of her mouth crinkled into a feral grin. "I eat little boys like you for breakfast."

"Now wait a darned minute." Heat rushed to his face. He was surprised he had any blood left outside his cock to do anything.

"Love to, but I can't or I'll be late for my next client." Kate pushed to her feet. "Nice to meet you…Devon." She walked slowly from the café, her hips swinging in a tantalizing rhythm.

Devon stared after her. Far from making things better, his tiny taste of Kate had done nothing but whet his appetite for more. He glanced at his wrist computer. Three more days until his doctor appointment. He bit his lower lip.

How was he going to make it seem coincidental when he showed up at her office? He drained his coffee and got to his feet.

Guess I'll have to tell her the truth. I can't get her out of my mind. If she throws me out on my ass, there's not much I can do about it.

~

KATE MADE HERSELF WALK SLOWLY. It wouldn't do for the man to think she was afraid of him, or onto him. It was the same man who'd followed her a few days before. The one who fucked her every night in her dreams. He was desperately attractive. She'd felt the heat of his arousal all the way across the café. If he'd done anything but settle at her table, she would've been shocked. Kate's nipples pressed against her lacy bra. Her pussy lips slipped and slid against one another. She'd nearly come when he met her gaze with his incredible dark eyes. It had taken all her restraint not to straddle his lap. It was surprising just how much sex happened in public places. She regaled her clients with titillating tales of public sex all the time to spur their arousal.

Devon, my ass.

She snorted. He'd lied about what he did. Maybe his name was phony too. Kate was nearly certain he was one of the super cops who rounded up shifters. But he didn't seem interested in rounding her up. No, if she was any judge of that sort of thing, he wanted her as much as she wanted him.

Kate turned her mind inward to her cat. *"What does he want with us?"*

"Let's fuck him and find out."

A laugh bubbled up from her belly. *"My practical other half."*

"You asked. It's not my fault you didn't like my answer."

Kate trotted up the steps to her office, activated the electronics, and let herself inside. She glanced at her wrist computer. No clients for a couple of hours.

Guess I lied to Devon too.

She made certain her door was locked and walked to the toy box she kept on the far side of the bed in her studio. Kate culled through it for her vibrating dildo and a butterfly to snap around her clit. She pulled her top over her head and slid out of her skirt. Devon's sharply boned face and broad shoulders formed in her imagination.

She fantasized him dropping his vest and pulling his shirt over his head. Bronzed skin stretched over shapely muscles. Dark nipples puckered with desire, he swept her into his arms and kissed her. Kate felt the hard planes of his chest push into her breasts.

Unsure how it happened, she ended up on her bed, legs spread. Kate clicked on the dildo and pushed it inside her, angling it to tease her G-spot. She clipped the butterfly over her clit and twanged its wings. The device pulsated. Whoever had designed it was clever. It only needed a nudge from time to time to keep stimulating her sensitive nub.

Kate's back arched like a bow. Her breath came fast. She tweaked her nipples with her free hand and mimicked fucking with the vibrating dildo. All the while, Devon was alive in her mind. He was the one fucking her. The one pulling her nipples. He had the most amazing cock. Long and thick, he filled her more thoroughly than anyone else ever had. Her hips thrust upward again and again. She moved the dildo faster.

"Now, goddamn it, now," she shrieked. Climax roared through her, shaking her to her core.

Kate's head lolled against the pillows. She gasped for air. Her clit still throbbed. She worked the butterfly, decided she needed more direct contact and replaced it with the tip of the vibrating dildo. The dark-haired stranger wrapped his arms around her. His lips closed on hers. He murmured he loved her, couldn't stop thinking about her. When he lowered his lips to suck her nipples, she came again, spasming so hard she was sure she'd pass out.

It was a while before she could breathe. "I have to see him again," she murmured. "If I don't, I'll never figure this out."

"Good call," her cat purred. *"How are we going to find him?"*

Kate rolled to a sitting position and got off the bed. She headed for the bathroom to rinse herself and her toys off. *"I don't think we need to worry about that,"* she replied. *"He seems pretty resourceful. I think he'll probably find us."*

CHAPTER 5

Devon stared at the placard next to the door reading, HENRY ADAMS, M.D. He was on the third floor of a medical arts building. His lips thinned to a hard line. He hated doctors, and avoided them whenever possible, but it was the only way to get in to see a surrogate. As it was, it had taken him nearly a week to secure an appointment. He wondered what people did who were truly ill. Devon yanked the door open and trod heavily to the front desk where he tapped on frosted glass.

"Your business, please," a disembodied voice came from a speaker. The glass panel—probably bulletproof—didn't budge.

"Devon Heartshorn. I have an appointment."

"Did you bring your paperwork?"

"Yes. Downloaded it from the vid feed like you said."

"Place it in the tray in front of you. Have a seat. Someone will be with you shortly."

Devon fidgeted in the hard plastic chair. "Shortly" turned out to be just over an hour.

"Mr. Heartshorn," blared from the speaker. "Proceed to the green door and place your palm on the pad."

So much for patient privacy, he thought wryly, glancing around the overflowing waiting room.

After weight, height, blood pressure, and a nurse asking questions—most of which he didn't answer—Devon was stuffed in an exam room the size of a large closet. Tired of sitting after his stint in the waiting room, he paced, two steps one direction, then back again.

Half an hour later a tall, thin, harried-looking man in his fifties pushed the door open, walked to the sink, and washed his hands. "Glad to meet you, Mr. Heartshorn," he said without looking at Devon. "What can I do for you today? My nurse said you were evasive when she asked you questions."

"I can wait until you finish with your hands."

Breath rattled through the doctor's teeth. He grabbed a paper towel and turned to face Devon. Tired brown eyes gazed out of a deeply lined face. Brown hair, turning gray, was cut short. "Okay. You have my undivided attention."

"Um, it's a little embarrassing..." Devon studied the stained tile floor. Even though he'd practiced at home in front of his bathroom mirror, he felt heat rise from the open neck of his shirt.

"Sex, eh?" Dr. Adams nodded knowingly. "I've pretty much heard it all, son. What is it? Do you think you caught something?"

Devon snorted. "Wish I could. See, I can't seem to..." He let his voice trail off.

"How long haven't you been able to have sex?" Dr. Adams was all business. "And is it that you can't get erections, or that you don't last long enough."

Devon felt his face get even warmer. "Uh, both. And it's always been this way, but I screwed up one marriage. I'd like to find a wife, and—"

The doctor waved him to silence. "Think I've got the picture. Just let me do a brief exam here." He snapped on a pair of gloves. "Want to be sure you don't have prostate problems. If that checks out, I think a few surrogate sessions should fix you right up."

"Huh? What's that?" Devon tried to sound naïve and clueless.

"Drop your pants and bend over." The doctor inserted a finger into Devon's anus and felt around. "Okay. Everything's good there." He dropped the gloves in a waste can and put on a fresh pair. "Now lay on the table for me." He bent over Devon and poked and prodded. "A surrogate is a woman who helps you with sexual problems." The doctor flashed a lascivious grin. "Sort of like a prostitute, but with a college degree in what makes men tick."

"Oh." Devon looked away. "How much does it cost?"

Dr. Adams shrugged. "They all have their own fee scales. Insurance won't cover it, even with a prescription from me. Best bet is to call around. The nurse will give you a list. Okay, Mr. Heartshorn. You're all done here. Don't think you need any labs today. Get dressed. My nurse will be in with an authorization from me and that list."

"Um, you won't have to tell my employer about this, will you?"

Dr. Adams looked human for the first time since he'd come into the exam room. "No. And I won't. Can't see where it would interfere with your job. Those are the only things I have to report. You're a cop. Your fellow officers would never let you live this down. No worries."

The door whooshed shut. Devon scrambled into his Levis and shoes and buttoned his shirt. The nurse showed up quickly. Minutes later, he ran down the building's steps three at a time, jubilant his ploy had worked. He had a way to see Kate. As soon as he could find an electronics store, he'd buy a nice, anonymous, throwaway wrist computer and call her.

Devon jogged to a seedy neighborhood and searched both sides of the street. Being a cop had some perks, since he had a general idea who sold what to whom. He ducked into a shop, looked over the electronic merchandise, and plunked down black market cash for an untraceable wrist computer preloaded with two hundred minutes, seventy-five texts, and fifty searches.

Devon punched numbers into the computer from an alleyway

next to the shop. Bums lined its sides, but they never gave him any problems. His size and obviously superb physical condition were quite a deterrent.

She answered on the second ring. "Kate Roman." It surprised him. He'd expected a recording.

"Uh, hi. My name is Heartshorn. I got a referral from Dr. Adams to see you. I, um, wanted to make an appointment. And I guess I need to know how much you charge."

Laughter tinkled against his ear. "Sure. I know Dr. Adams. Let's see. I had a cancellation this afternoon at five. Or there's three tomorrow. Would either of those work for you?"

"Your fees?" Devon tried desperately to act like a normal client.

"Sure. First visit is seven hundred fifty credits. It includes a full assessment and a report back to your referring doctor. Subsequent visits are six hundred fifty credits."

Devon whistled. Steep. He thought about the hundred fifty credits Huong had charged. It didn't matter; he would've paid any amount to get Kate with her clothes off. She dogged his dreams every night. He wasn't sure how the hell he'd be able to fake erectile dysfunction, but he'd cross that bridge when he got to it.

"If that's too much," she said, her voice kind, "I can give you the names of some women who charge less."

"No," he blurted. "It's fine. You said you had a cancellation at five?"

"Uh-huh."

"Okay. I'll take it. Bye."

"Wait. Don't you need my address and directions?"

"Aren't they on the sheet the doctor gave me?" It wouldn't do to tell her he knew exactly where her office was.

"I don't think so. They shouldn't be. Do me a favor and check. You can tell me when I see you. I'm in a pale blue Victorian. The address is…"

Devon floated down the street. This was working better than he'd hoped. He was off work today and traveling on foot. Since he was new and trying to earn his chops, he would have stopped in at the station house, but he couldn't risk getting snared in an emergency. Besides, it was only about two hours until his appointment.

Deciding to splurge, he walked into a sit-down restaurant. No self-serve cafés for him today. Obviously successful businessmen dressed in suits and ties were scattered through the establishment in small groups. They looked askance at his worn jeans, pressed linen shirt, and the leather vest he rarely left home without, before quickly averting their gazes.

A waitress wearing an über-short shirt and tiny top hurried over to him on ridiculously high heels. Bleached blonde hair frizzed around her face. Breasts spilled over the top of her low neckline. He caught a whiff of stale cigarette smoke mixed with sweat and cheap cologne.

Damn. Those IV infusions really amped up his senses.

"Did you have a reservation, sir?" she purred.

"No, but I see lots of empty tables." Sensing she was about to tell him to leave, he flashed his cop creds.

"Oh, I see," she murmured. "I'm sure I can find you something."

"I want that table." He pointed to a choice spot near a window.

"Certainly. I'll have someone set it."

"Great. Bring a menu while you're at it." Devon loped to the table and settled his oversized frame into a carved wooden chair. After a few moments, the low drone of conversation picked up again. He figured folk would ignore him, and they did.

He lingered over a salad, steak, bottle of red wine, coffee, and desert until it was nearly time for his appointment. His eyes widened at the bill, and he shook his head. It had been an exceptional meal, but scarcely worth five hundred credits. San Bernardino didn't have such a sharp demarcation between haves and have-nots. He tapped a few keys on his wrist computer and wrote the code on the bill. He assumed a tip was added in to the total. He didn't want to risk leaving black market cash on the table.

He pushed to his feet and snorted. Didn't matter if he pissed off the waitress. It was unlikely he'd be back. He made good money, but it wasn't good enough to indulge at places like this, at least not very often.

His blood thrummed as he walked briskly toward Kate's office. Anticipation zipped through him. His cock surged against the front of his pants. He moved it so his zipper wasn't rubbing against it and told it to calm down. It wouldn't do to show up at her door with a raging hard-on. With her enhanced senses, she'd be sure to smell his arousal, never mind the front of his pants being tented like he was smuggling a boomerang.

He tried counting backward. Next he tried solving complex equations. Neither worked. His cock was insistent. It wanted Kate, and it wanted her bad. He mentally rehearsed a slightly different story, using premature ejaculation as his presenting issue. That would let him sidestep having an erection on her front stoop. His heart thudded. His mouth was dry. He walked up her steps and rang the bell.

KATE SMILED TO HERSELF. Her newest client was right on time. She appreciated punctuality. Kate padded to her front door, flipped the safety viewer, and froze. It was him. Holy Christ! Her nipples peaked. Her breathing quickened. She dreamed about him almost every night. Hot, graphic dreams of them doing just about everything two people could do to one another. Quite different from the quiet, controlled sex in her surrogate studio. She'd added twice-daily masturbation sessions since he sat at her table in the café.

Calm down. If he wanted to arrest me, I'd be gone by now.

I don't know that. Not for sure, another voice posited dryly. It was the only dry thing about her. Liquid slicked her thighs.

"*Oooooh,*" her cat purred. "*Looks like he found us. What are you waiting for? Get him in here.*"

He rang the bell again. Kate felt trapped, but more than trapped, she was hotter than she'd been in years. She rubbed her thighs against one another and almost came. Her cat's opinion aside, common sense told her to make a run for the back door. It would take her down an interior staircase and out into the alleyway. That part of her mind screamed in protest when her hand snaked out to disengage the locks.

The man smiled at her. Warm, dark eyes crinkled at the corners. He held out a hand. "I'm Devon Heartshorn. For a minute there, I was afraid I'd gotten the wrong date or time or address. Say—" his brows drew together "—you're the one I ran into the other day at the restaurant. What a coincidence."

Like hell it is.

The lie pinged sourly against her magic. Kate stood with her mouth hanging open. She finally shook his hand. Words were beyond her; they stuck in her throat.

Devon's smile faded. "Um, look, if you're not feeling well or something, maybe we could reschedule."

Disgust with herself roiled through her. When had she turned into such an insipid coward? Her style had always been to meet things head on. She sucked in a steadying breath, followed by another. "No. I'm fine. I was just, uh, surprised. Come in. Follow me right over here. I have a terminal where you can enter your information." She pointed to the corner desk.

Kate usually gave her new clients space, but she stood right behind Devon's ramrod straight back once he settled in the chair and watched him enter data. "There." She tapped the screen with the nail of her index finger. "It asked for your occupation. You left it blank. Why?" She folded her arms across her chest and waited.

"Didn't it say at the top of the form I could leave things blank?"

Damn!

"Yes, it did say that, but most men are proud of what they do. Part of your first visit is me deciding if I'll accept you as a client." She hurried on. "A lot of men think visiting me is like hiring a prostitute. It's not. Trust between us is essential, or the relationship won't work for you, and you'll just be wasting your money. If you don't even trust me enough to tell me how you earn a living, well, I'm not terribly hopeful."

He turned the chair around so he faced her and spread his hands. "How about if you pull up a chair?" His face looked earnest, not threatening. She saw pleading in the depths of his eyes.

"Okay." Something with nasty claws walked up her back. Was it paranoia, or a genuine warning? For once, her cat was silent. Kate sensed it within her, watchful and waiting.

She reached out with her magic before settling a chair across from him. Not too close. She was edgy, ready to fight for her life if she had to. Despite that, her lust hadn't abated. Not one whit. Her body craved him. It didn't care if he was out to get her.

"Let's start with this." She locked gazes with him. "About a week ago, you followed me when I walked to work. Why?" Before he could answer, she hurried on. "And I'll be a blue monkey if you showing up at the café where I eat lunch every day was accidental."

He set his jaw in a hard line, and a muscle danced beneath one eye. "Guess I need to tell you. You'll find out soon enough once my clothes are off and you see the duty tattoos. I'm a cop. Just started working for the city, but I've been a cop for a long time. I'm part of the task force that's supposed to hunt down shif—, er, people like you."

She leapt to her feet and backed away, intent on putting as much distance as she could between her and Devon Heartshorn.

"No." He was on his feet too. "Please don't run away. I told my captain he was wrong about you."

She cocked her head to one side. He'd told her the truth. The words pinged clean against her magic. "Why would you do that? You said on my form, you'd only been here three months. Usually new hires want to make a good impression."

Color rose from the open neck of his shirt and stained his coppery skin, giving it a bronze tint. "Because I think you're beautiful. I couldn't stand the thought of you not being free."

"It's more than not being free. It's being dead." She squared her shoulders and tossed her hair over them. "Surely you must know they're killing us before they book us into prison." She laughed bitterly. "Really cuts down on the overhead if they don't have to feed us."

His eyes widened. "No. I didn't know that. What about the Human Rights Commission?"

"Haven't you heard? Shifters aren't classified as human anymore." She slammed a fist into her open palm. No matter how much she wanted to fuck him, he really needed to leave. And right now. "Look—"

"Please." He extended a hand toward her. "My mother was a shifter, half anyway. She died in prison. I—I've never felt so confused in my life." He turned away. "Sorry," he mumbled. "Shouldn't have told you that. It's not your problem."

Compassion battled briefly with apprehension and won. "You work for the people who killed your kin. Christ, Devon, no wonder you're conflicted. Do you really have sexual problems, or did you just want to see me?"

He didn't say anything. Kate made a snap decision. He hadn't entered any of the data he'd typed. She crossed the room, leaned over the computer, and pushed cancel.

"It's more than wanted to see you," he said, his voice low and thrumming with emotion. "I haven't been able to think about anything but you since I followed you that day. You're in my dreams when I sleep and in my head when I'm awake." He closed the distance between them and spun her to face him, keeping his hands on her shoulders. The intensity in his gaze burned all the way into her soul. "I even hired a hooker, but when I was inside her, all I saw was you."

A well-protected place deep within Kate melted. She wound her arms around his waist and met his gaze with a ferocity born of denied need. "I've had the same problem. Ever since I caught a glimpse of you through my windows, I haven't been able to get you out of my mind." She snorted, grabbed handfuls of his shirt, and clung to it. "It's been good for my clients. I'm sure they've thought they turned into Joe Stud, but I've been pretending each of them was you."

She pressed her breasts against his chest. Her nipples hardened, sending electric jolts to her pussy. He felt right in her arms, like he belonged there. His high, tight ass made her want to squeeze it. Kate's breath clotted in her throat. She couldn't wait to get his clothes off.

A groan tore out of him. His face flushed. A hell of an erection pushed against her stomach. Kate's cat purred. Its feline heat poured through her, adding to her arousal. She dropped her hands to his wonderful ass and pulled him tight against her.

CHAPTER 6

*D*evon closed his arms around her back. He bent his head and kissed her, tentative at first, then harder when she clutched him and opened her mouth to his probing tongue. He tasted sweet, like cinnamon and wine.

No wonder I'm so attracted to him. He has shifter blood.

"Shifter blood. Shifter blood," the cat echoed.

Kate pushed her body against his and dropped a hand between them to rub his cock where it strained against the fabric of his faded jeans.

He broke away from their kiss and made a sound like a large, satisfied cat purring. He put a hand over one of her breasts and traced her erect nipple with a fingertip. "Any chance of getting these clothes off? I've spent hours imagining what you look like without them."

Kate grinned. "Funny, I was just thinking the same thing. Come on." She grabbed his hand and led him into the bedroom, then stopped just inside the door. She'd never used this room for anything other than work.

What the hell? If they're after me, I may not be here much longer, anyway. I might need to go to ground somewhere...

"What?" He wrapped his arms around her from behind and pulled her against his chest. His hands closed over her breasts, rubbing, touching, teasing.

"Nothing. This has always been my studio. Sex is for the men first, and maybe for me if it doesn't interfere with—"

"Would you like me to take you somewhere else?" His deep voice rumbled next to her ear. He kissed her earlobe and strung kisses down her neck while his fingers twirled her nipples into stiff peaks. His cock pressed against her bottom.

Heat exploded in her crotch. She shook her head. "No." Her voice was thick with passion. "I don't want to wait."

"Neither do I." He pulled her emerald green top over her head and turned her to face him. She heard a sharp intake of breath. "You are the most beautiful creature I've ever laid eyes on." He growled deep in his throat and filled his hands with her breasts again. Kate moaned. She pushed his vest off his shoulders. He shrugged out of it. She went to work on the buttons of his shirt, her legs almost too unsteady to hold her upright.

He moved from her breasts to her hips, and shoved her skirt down. It puddled on the floor where she stepped around it. After stopping and just staring, admiration stark on his face, he buried a hand between her legs and rubbed her passion-slick clit.

"Bed." She pointed, then saw he still had his jeans on. She undid the snap and zipper. His cock sprang out, and she gasped. Even through the lust-heat fuzzing her brain, it was the biggest, most amazing cock she'd ever seen. Full and hot and hard. She closed a hand partway round it and groaned in anticipation. Reaching behind her, she grabbed a condom from the bedside table and unrolled it onto his wonderful erection.

Kate wanted him inside her more than she'd ever wanted anything. She didn't think she'd last past a couple of strokes, but it didn't matter. She rubbed her pussy against his hand then backed toward the bed, threw herself down, spread her legs, and opened her arms.

Devon moved between her thighs, took hold of himself, and guided his cock inside her. She felt herself stretch to accommodate him and raised her legs, locking them around his hips. He supported himself on his arms and gazed at her with desire blazing at the bottom of his dark eyes.

Kate understood. Being a shifter was like that. No matter how much sex you had with humans, you still lusted after your own kind. She put her hands on his hips and rocked herself against him. Her clit was on fire. She rubbed it against the base of his wonderful cock until it exploded. Lust seared her, marked her, and her muscles clenched around him over and over.

His gaze never left her body as her vault convulsed around him. "So beautiful," he murmured. "I wanted to watch you come just like I do in my dreams." He moved a little, drew partway out, and pressed himself deep inside her again. "I was worried I'd come too soon."

She laughed. "I wasn't. I knew you'd be hard pressed to beat me to the draw. You've been in my dreams too. But the real thing is ever so much better." She thrust her hips upward. "I want you to fuck me. Come on, Devon. Hard and fast. I want to feel you come inside me."

He made that wonderful sound again, low in the back of his throat. He withdrew until just the tip of him teased her and drove himself home, then did it again. He leaned down so his face was next to hers, breath hot against her neck. After teasing kisses on her cheeks and eyelids, he closed his mouth over hers and kissed her deeply.

Kate met him stroke for stroke, feeling another climax build deep in her belly. She was so lost in passion, she almost didn't notice soft fur sprouting against her legs and arms. Her eyes snapped open. At first, she thought he was shifting, and then she understood she was shifting right along with him. Their fur, his slightly more golden, mingled together, and her vision was altered because she looked through cat eyes with their slit pupils. She hadn't ever shifted spontaneously before.

She broke away from their kiss, talking while she still could. "Holy crap! Devon."

He opened his eyes, pushed up onto his arms, and looked at her. Something in her tone must have gotten through. He stopped moving. He cock twitched inside her, heavy with need. "What? Condom's still—"

"Ssht, it will be okay. I don't want to ruin this with a bunch of talk. You're shifting. Your eyes are unbelievable. I'm shifting too. We'll finish this in our other forms."

A panicked look washed over his face. His gaze darted to his body. He yanked away from her, jumped off the bed, and stood, panting. "Not possible. I don't have enough shifter blood." He shook his head. "My eyes are all funny." He flicked at tawny fur growing thicker by the minute on his torso and limbs. "I don't even know what I'll be. I mean, I've never…"

Kate got to her feet. "Just let it happen. It's easy. The most natural thing in the world. Let everything go. As far gone as you are, you couldn't stop it now if you tried." She grinned. "Looking at your fur, I'm betting you're a mountain cat just like me."

"Will we still be able to talk?"

She nodded. "Yes, but in our minds." Kate sucked in a breath. She reached for her animal form, completing the transformation. Once she had her paws under her, she turned her butt toward Devon and arched her back suggestively.

A wonderfully feline growl sounded from behind her, low and throaty. Kate's whiskers twitched. Nothing like a male cat on the prowl. She didn't have to look to know his shift was complete. She braced herself and took the weight of his body, glorying in it. Teeth closed over her neck where it joined her shoulder. It had been over a hundred years since she'd had a shifter partner. Maybe that was why her control had gotten away from her.

Just as outrageously outsized as he'd been when he was human, he plumbed her, barbs and all. She hissed and whined her pleasure, writhing against him. His cock jumped inside her and jumped again.

His teeth bit deeper. He let go and roared his passion and delight. Her own climax rocked her, rippling along her nerve endings. The barbs on his cock ramped up her pleasure tenfold. Nothing was quite as sizzling and untamed as shifted sex.

Nothing.

It took time for him to slip from her body. The barbs were mildly uncomfortable when he withdrew, but what they'd shared was worth it. Once he was free, she turned to look at him. A husky purr reverberated from deep in her belly—the feline equivalent of a wolf whistle.

"Wow. You're even more gorgeous as a cat than you were as a human."

He shook his head back and forth and shifted his weight from paw to paw, obviously uncomfortable with his four-legged stance. *"I —I need to be human again. Now. Tell me what to do."*

"Think of your human body. Visualize it and you'll be there. Once you get used to—"

The edges of his cat body shimmered. Kate gave her own body the command to shift right along with his.

"Christ!" Devon sank into a heap on the floor. He tugged what was left of the condom off himself and dropped it on the rug. "What the fuck happened to it? It's shredded."

"Cat cocks have barbs." At the desperate look on his face, she hastened to add, "Hey, it will be all right." Kate sat across from him, leaned forward, and stroked his thigh. "Really it will. And it will get easier to change over—"

"I don't want it to get easier." Anguish rode beneath his words. "In fact, I don't ever want it to happen again."

Understanding crashed into her. Of course he wouldn't. He'd just transitioned from one of the hunters to one of the hunted. She took a measured breath and chose her words carefully. "I think you shifted this time because you were excited. Strong emotions can force a shift. That's how most of us learned to shift as children. Someone baited us until we found our animal forms. After you find it once, it's easier the next time. Soon it's second nature."

"But I don't have enough blood to shift into anything," he protested. "I'm only a quarter."

She shrugged. "I don't know what to say. You are pretty old for an initial shift. Now that I think about it, I've never heard of something like this happening—"

"That does not make me feel better," he snapped.

Of course it wouldn't. Kate kicked herself and took a deep breath. "Is there anything that's changed lately?"

He slammed his forehead against a hand. "Of course. Stupid of me not to..."

Kate waited, but he didn't say anything else. Finally, she prodded, "...stupid of you not to what?"

He showed her the inside of his forearm where a bruise was fading. "The police force insisted I take a series of intravenous infusions. It was a prerequisite for working here. I never asked what was in them." A muscle in his jaw jerked. "Figured I wouldn't understand all that chemical mumbo-jumbo anyway."

He blew out a breath. "They give us stuff to alter our genetics when we sign on as officers. It creates an edge in the field, helps keep us alive. I got that series of shots fifteen years ago. Whatever was in the recent infusions was supposed make us more sensitive to shifters."

"Humph." She narrowed her eyes in thought. "Looks like when the drug combines with shifter blood, it strengthens it. Once upon a time, scientists would've wanted to know things like that."

"I'm sure as hell not going to tell them." He dropped his head into a hand. It muffled his next words. "You said strong emotions can make me shift."

"Yes, but you'll learn to control it."

"How long will that take? Police work is nothing but strong emotions." He raised his head and locked his dark, tortured gaze onto hers. "Fear, anger, pity..." He ticked them off on his fingers. "That's just for starters. There's not a day on the force where I don't end up feeling strongly about something."

"I don't know how long. I learned when I was young. All of us have our first shift right around puberty. It might be easier then, or harder. I just don't know." She spread her hands in front of her. "I'm sorry. I know it seems like the end of the world—"

"It is the end—of my world, anyway," he growled. "May as well stop by the station house and turn in my badge. It's better than being in the middle of working a crime scene with a partner and turning into a mountain lion." He curled his hands into fists where they rested in his lap.

An idea took root. "Maybe you could work for our side—" she began.

He shook his head. Hair flew around his face. "I can't talk about this anymore. None of it." He lurched to his feet and stumbled into his clothes. His eyes looked haunted. "Is there a back way out of here? I don't want to see any more people than I absolutely have to. Not the shape I'm in."

She nodded, got to her feet, and wrapped herself in a robe. "This way." She wanted to talk to him, reassure him, but he had such a closed look on his face, she thought it best not to try. He wouldn't hear her, anyway.

She led him into her small, personal room behind the bedroom and ran her hand over the electronic lock. "It's just down the stairs. The door at the bottom unlocks along with this one."

Devon turned to her. He pulled her roughly against him. "This is my own fault." His voice rumbled against her hair. "I wanted you so much, I broke all the rules." His arms tightened. "Don't worry, Kate. No matter what happens, I won't turn you in."

He kissed her forehead, spun, and ran down the steps. Once she heard the bottom door close, she activated the lock and walked slowly back to the bedroom. It smelled like sex, shifter sex. Raw and musky. Her eyes welled. He was the best, the most perfect shifter she'd met in several human lifetimes.

"He's our mated one!" her cat crowed. *"We have to go after him and bring him back."*

"No, it can't be. You're just lonely—like me."

"I'm right," the cat insisted. *"That's why you shifted spontaneously."*

Kate ignored her. Shifter mates were scarce as hen's teeth. It was the reason so many of them married humans. Besides, Devon didn't want her, not anymore. He had when he'd shown up on her front porch, and pretty badly. If the price for sex with her was shifting, though, all bets were off. She'd seen it in his eyes: horror and disgust with what he'd become. No, if he were truly her shifter mate, he'd have welcomed her with open arms.

"You're wrong," the cat insisted. *"You caught him at a bad moment. Give him some time to get used to the idea—"*

"Stop. Just stop. How could my mated one be a cop? They're the enemy. Or haven't you been paying attention?"

The cat subsided into a grumbling snarl.

Kate went on autopilot and stripped the bed. It was either that or curl in a ball on the floor and howl her misery. With her arms full of linens, she started for the small washer and dryer. His scent filled her nostrils. She buried her nose in the sheets and changed her mind about washing them—at least for now. If his smell was all she had left of him, she wanted to hang onto it. Her heart ached. So did her pussy, but it was a sweet pain.

Kate did a slipshod job making the bed. A few minutes later, she stood in the shower. An idea shot through her as hot water sluiced down her body. She didn't understand all the ramifications, but there had to be some. Once she was dry and dressed, she settled at her computer terminal and called the underground on their secure frequency. Max's face appeared on her screen.

She sketched out what had happened with Devon. It wasn't easy because Max kept interrupting. A tall, lean man with Germanic features and shoulder-length blond hair, Maximillian Sigayev gestured with his hands while he talked. His blue eyes were intent, gaze never leaving her. In his animal form, he was a Russian wolf with an almost white coat and the same sky-blue eyes. He steepled his fingers. "So there's a drug that could make us stronger. And make more of us from those with weak, mixed blood."

Kate nodded. "That's what it looks like. I'm not certain how old Devon is since I wiped his data off my computer, but he has to be somewhere between his mid-thirties and forty. A first shift at that age is unheard of."

"I agree." He eyed her. "So long as you called me, how is everything else? Food supplies holding up?"

Kate snaked her tongue out of her mouth and licked her lips. She hadn't told the underground that Tara, Joe, and Mike were gone. Apparently the three had done a good job hiding if Max still assumed they were with her. "There have been a few, er, changes."

A corner of his mouth turned down. "Spill it, Roman. I don't have all day."

"...so, I left them in the woods with most of the food. It wasn't like I had much of a choice. They would've left anyway."

Max nodded. "I understand. Don't blame yourself. They haven't hit my radar, so they must be all right, at least for now. I have to run. Your intel about the drug may prove to be our salvation."

"How so?"

"Not sure just yet, but you might have struck gold, Miss Roman. I need to run it past a couple of our biological scientists."

The screen flickered and grayed out. Kate sat and stared at it for a while before she got to her feet. She did her usual cursory check that her office was ready for her next client before letting herself out the door. It was dark outside. She glanced at her wrist computer.

Sheesh. How'd it get to be eight o'clock?

There were several unopened messages, but she'd tend to them later. If she tarried, she'd miss the last bus. Taxis were ridiculously expensive. Kate dropped her wrist computer into a pocket and lengthened her stride.

As she jogged toward the bus stop, she thought about Devon. He'd been even dishier in the flesh than in her dreams. His shifter status was like icing on an already toothsome cake. She felt torn. The attraction between them was strong. On his side as well or he wouldn't have bent his standards to buy time with her.

I've got to stop living in Never-Never Land. He doesn't want me anymore. Couldn't wait to get away... And even if he did, it would be foolish for me to link my star to a cop.

"I tell you," the cat growled. *"He is our mated one. Stop fighting it."*

"Be quiet. You'll get us killed. He's a cop. His job is to capture us."

Kate waited for some pushback, but the cat was apparently done talking.

Her thoughts returned to Devon. His professional life was all about following orders. As law enforcement, it would almost have to be. Despite his assurance he'd never turn her in, she wasn't certain his ingrained sense of duty wouldn't trip him up—and snare her right along with him.

She waved her arms at the bus and ran hard. The doors swooshed open, accompanied by a dirty look from the attendant. The buses didn't need drivers. The city had run them without any human assistance until homeless took up residence in the public transportation system. Between crapping in the buses and heckling people who simply wanted a ride from Point A to Point B, bums had practically disabled the system. It took a while, but the powers that be decided it was cheaper to assign a person to each bus.

She flashed her wrist computer app at the attendant and ran her screen over the glass. It beeped and debited ten credits from her account. Kate glanced up the aisle. Not so many people tonight. She worked her way to a window seat, fell into it, and tried to empty her mind of Devon.

Just when she thought she'd succeeded, her cat piped up. *"He's only a cop because he didn't understand he was one of us."*

CHAPTER 7

*D*evon felt like someone had kicked him in the stomach. He tried to ignore the pain, but it had done nothing but get worse since he left Kate. His mouth flooded with saliva.

He doubled over and vomited into a trashcan on a street corner. Spasms wracked his body. He heaved again and again until the only thing left was bile. Feeling shaky, he drew the back of a hand across his mouth and shambled toward his little house. Passersby gave him a wide berth while he hurled his guts out. Probably thought he had some horrible disease. Or was a junkie.

He tried not to think about anything, but images of mountain lions rose to taunt him. He saw himself mounted behind Kate, also in her cat form, thrusting into her. Ill and shaky as he was, damn if his cock didn't twitch.

What kind of sick son of a bitch am I?

He glanced around him. Thank God it was only another half block home. It had taken nearly two hours to travel what should've taken half that time. He wanted to lock the door and never come out. Never.

He dragged his body up the steps, dredged the key out of a pocket, and let himself inside. Feeling hollow and out of control,

Devon bent over the kitchen sink to rinse the taste of sickness from his mouth. He fell into a kitchen chair, peeled a banana, and ate it. Maybe it wouldn't come right back up. He had to eat something; he was dizzy.

He stared at his hands. His vision blurred, and they turned into paws with tawny fur and long, lethal, curved claws. He blinked, and they were just hands again. He thought about trying to shift so he could develop some sort of control over what it felt like, but discarded the idea. What if he screwed up and couldn't get back? His heartbeat sounded loud in his ears, telling him how rattled he was.

"No." He spoke aloud to calm himself. "If I try to shift, I should be in the hills. At least there are other mountain lions there. If I couldn't find my human form again, there'd be game to hunt."

The banana seemed to be staying put. He ate another and put water on the stove to heat for coffee. He hated microwaves. He'd found the stove in a falling-down second hand store and wired the electrical lines in tandem to accept its two hundred twenty volt plug.

Devon massaged his temples. There was so much he didn't understand. He couldn't look up the sort of things he needed to know about being a shifter on the vid feed. No privacy. Anyone could track his browsing history. His mother had two sisters, shifters like her. And his grandmother was still alive. Her shifter blood was pure. Somewhere in the back of his mind he recalled shifters lived a long time. He didn't know exactly how long since they never talked about things like that—at least not with him.

He spooned instant coffee and sugar into a cup and poured water over it, stirring. He pulled the anonymous wrist computer he'd purchased earlier from his vest. Lots of minutes left on it. He wondered if any of his mother's people would talk with him— assuming he could even find them. They'd gone into hiding and moved frequently. He hadn't seen any of them, except at his mother's funeral, since the edict went into effect.

Devon drank some coffee and grimaced. Even if he could reach his aunts or grandmother, they'd probably laugh and tell him it was divine justice he'd turned into one of them. He thought about calling Kate, even tapped in her number before chickening out. He sent her a text message instead. It was easier that way. If she ignored it, he'd know…

Well, what would I know?

That she doesn't want anything to do with me, he answered himself.

Devon stared at the computer's blank display for several minutes. His heart ached. He'd hoped she'd text back. All he'd asked was if they could talk, that he had questions.

"Guess that answers that," he muttered and slugged back half the cup of coffee. Caffeine would help. He waited for it to jolt him out of his funk. It didn't happen fast enough, so he drained the rest of the cup.

He grappled for his other wrist computer to find his aunts' and grandmother's numbers. He thought about who was least likely to be judgmental. It occurred to him they might not believe him, might think he was playing some sort of underhanded cop trick to gather classified information. He laid both computers on the table.

No time for a trip to San Bernardino. He didn't have any vacation or sick time on the books. That took six months to accrue. He considered quitting—again. It would be the kiss of death for his law enforcement career.

What career? He asked himself bitterly. *I won't have a career once they find out what I am. Or a life, if they have any say about it.*

The implications of that sank in and bit deep. What he'd told Kate was true. His life had altered radically in the seconds it took for fur to sprout from his sides. Never mind the tail and claws and lengthened incisors.

Devon clapped a hand over his mouth and bolted for the bathroom mirror. He skinned back his upper lip and inspected his eyeteeth. His eyes narrowed. They were longer, but it wasn't that noticeable. Still, he couldn't be a cop anymore. It would only be a matter of time before the brass found him out.

His gaze roved down his body. It felt alien. Strange. Had anything else changed? With his jaw set in a hard line, he stripped off his clothes and examined himself, using the wall mirror and a handheld one for his backside. He exhaled sharply, not realizing he'd been holding his breath. Nothing else was different.

Not yet, anyway.

He flipped on the taps in the shower. May as well clean up. Some shreds of condom were stuck in his foreskin, so he peeled it back to loosen them. Kate's scent filled his nose. A wave of longing so intense it undid him made his cock spring to attention. He ignored it and stepped into the shower.

His dick was still hard, curved against his stomach, when he turned the water off. He dried himself, hands lingering at his crotch. Finally, he gave in and leaned against the bathroom wall. He saw his reflection in the mirror as his hand closed over his shaft. He knew what he needed. His hand pumped, slowly at first, and then his grip tightened and he worked himself harder. His muscles tensed.

Kate with all her splendid hair unbound appeared before him. She straddled him and thrust her hips against him. His breathing quickened. He was close. He imagined placing his mouth over Kate's nipple and sucking hard. Her body writhed under him. She pushed his head lower. He strung kisses down her flat stomach and sucked on her clit. Kate's lusty abandon unfolding behind his closed lids intensified his desire. Just a few more strokes...

His balls tightened. His cock bucked in his hand. Semen arced out of him, splattering the floor. He came hard. It surprised him since he'd just come a few hours before. After all, at thirty-eight he was well past the age when he'd gone around with a perpetual hard-on and could come half a dozen times a day.

Panting hard, he opened his eyes and grabbed a towel to clean up the mess. It slipped out of his hand. He bent to retrieve it and glanced downward. *Shit!* No wonder he'd dropped the towel. He didn't have hands anymore. Paws with fur and claws mocked him. He looked at his belly, at a line of fur gathered near his groin. It moved upward as he stared at himself.

Kate did this to him. Emotions made him shift. He straightened. Bile rose, filling his mouth with a sour taste. He stood frozen in place, waiting.

What the fuck? I'm just standing here like a goddamned idiot. There's got to be something I can do. Something proactive—

His wrist computer chimed—the regular one. He had no idea what the black market computer even sounded like. He made a dash for the kitchen and snapped it up awkwardly. "Heartshorn."

"We have a situation." His captain's voice was sharp with urgency. "Know it's your day off, but we need everyone we can scare up."

Devon opened his mouth to say he was quitting, but his captain started talking again. "Need you at Market and Fifth. Wear your body armor and riot gear."

"What happened?" In spite of himself, Devon was back in cop mode. He glanced at his body, noting he was human again. Maybe, if he caught the shift soon enough…

"The lab we use was robbed. Whoever planned this was a pro. Staged a riot and used it as cover. That part of things is still going strong. Good thing you're done with your treatments. Some scumbag stole every drop of our stock. It takes a while to make."

Devon's instincts went on high alert. He didn't know for certain, but he suspected Kate had something to do with the robbery. Shifters would want the advantage the drug gave them. Hell, if it pushed him over the edge, who knew what it would do to a fully vetted shifter? Plus, they could use it to swell their ranks with people like him.

"You still there, Heartshorn?"

"Yup. Still here. On my way, Captain."

He dressed as fast as he could, given all the layers he had to put on. Devon was disgusted with himself for not just quitting, but it went against the grain. Fellow officers' lives were on the line. The least he could do was help.

He'd just buckled his laser gun belt into place when his other computer squawked like a dying chicken. He glanced at the display. His eyes widened. A jolt of joy rocked him. Kate. She'd texted him back.

Call now. I'm home. Sorry. Didn't look at w.c. earlier.

He brought up a submenu and punched redial. Even though he hadn't actually called before, the computer held a record of the number he'd texted to. She picked up on the first ring.

"Devon?" She sounded tentative, wary.

"Yeah, it's me. I have lots of questions and not very much time."

"Okay. I'll help if I can."

"When I left you, I got really sick—"

"It's probably gone now," she interrupted. "Happens to all of us the first time we shift. Sorry. Didn't think to warn you. Frankly, I was just as surprised as you by what happened. Wasn't thinking all that straight."

"I got called in. I'm on my way to quell a riot downtown. Is there anything I can do to keep from shifting?"

"There are…warning signs. They're subtle and you might not notice them, but your hearing and sense of smell become more acute." She hesitated. "I'm guessing you have at least some shifter magic. We all have it. It will take time to teach you to manipulate it, but—"

"Kate." He heard desperation in his voice and tried to modulate it. "I really am rushed. If I notice my senses getting sharper, what do I do?"

"Visualize your human body. Anchor yourself to it."

"How? It's like you're speaking another language. Look, I'm sorry to bother you. I thought about calling my mother's family, but I figured they'd spit in my face. You're the only other shifter I know."

A sigh jangled through the cellular system. "The best thing

would be for me to show you some things. They're almost impossible to describe."

He checked the time. "I'm not sure when I'll be done working. Depends how bad things are and I won't know until I get there. If I can get free in two or three hours, where can I find you?"

There was a long silence. So long he checked the display to make certain they were still connected. "I'm not certain it's wise to tell you where I live. I'm paranoid enough about cops trapping me here—"

His heart constricted, but he understood her need for self-preservation. "Don't blame you. Gotta run. I won't bother you again."

"Wait!"

He moved the finger poised above the end call icon.

"Text me when you get free. I'll meet you at my office."

A warm glow started in his belly. Maybe she cared about him after all—at least a little. "Thanks, Kate."

She laughed. "Hope I live long enough to not regret this. Um, Devon."

"Yes?"

"You can't dance on both sides of the street. It won't work, at least not for very long."

The phone icon blinked out on the display. She'd ended the call. He glanced at his hand, horrified to see fur and claws again. Not as bad as in the bathroom, but obvious enough if anyone was looking at him. Strong emotions... Even if she didn't care about him, he cared about her. A whole lot, from the looks of things. He took a deep breath, blew it out, and inhaled a second time. He visualized himself as human, human, human, goddamn it. The next time he looked at his hand, it was skin and nails again.

"Well, hey," he murmured. "That wasn't so bad. If I can just keep track of my body, maybe I can fake my way through this riot." Her words about dancing on both sides of the street bounced in his head. He shoved them aside and hurried out the door. Adrenaline hummed through his blood. He loved fighting bad guys. It was the best part of being a cop.

An unpleasant thought intruded as he got into his patrol vehicle. At least according to the governmental directive about shifters, he'd just changed sides.

And become the enemy he'd taken an oath to eradicate.

~

KATE STARED at the wrist computer display. Her stomach tied itself into a knot. She didn't have good feelings about what Devon was trying to do. He was living his old life, not yet understanding it wasn't possible. Some shifters had tried to be double agents at the front end of the purge against them. It hadn't worked. As far as she knew, they'd all been caught and killed.

"*It's the same thing you're doing,*" her cat snarled. "*Denying reality. He's denying what he is now, and you're denying he's our mated one.*"

"*Jesus Christ! Whose side are you on? Don't we have enough problems without your nattering on about 'mated one, mated one?'*"

"*I'm on our side.*" The cat's voice was smug.

Kate blew out a worried breath. She'd heard about the riot. It had been on the screens mounted all around the bus. She'd used her wrist computer to tap into the frequency and listened for a while.

According to the broadcaster, some terrorist group had broken into a government lab, using the riot for cover. No sketches of the terrorists were available, but people were advised to stay home, lock their doors, and not open them unless they were certain they knew who was outside. Traffic had been rerouted, so it had taken her longer than usual to get home.

Kate's wrist computer LED blinked red. The underground frequency. Blinking red meant she should tune her desktop computer to the underground's secure channel. Far from an electronics whiz, she didn't totally understand why the vid feed could be scrambled more effectively than the wrist computer, but she mounted the stairs to her bedroom and study.

Her house wasn't large, but it was cozy. The main floor held a generous living room with a stone fireplace and picture windows with leaded glass panes. An old-fashioned kitchen sported a real stove and a small oak dinette sitting off to one side. The upstairs had a wonderful bathroom with a claw foot tub in addition to her sleeping and work space. Tubs like hers weren't legal anymore. They used too much water, but so far the city hadn't done a door-to-door inspection.

She flicked her hand over her computer to move it from sleep to wake mode. The wall screen flickered to life. Max had already begun talking.

"...thanks to one of our operatives, we now have access to a substance that may well enhance our powers. Stupid of the government to centralize everything." Max laughed harshly and waved a dismissive hand. "Made it easy to locate our objective. Our scientists are working on determining its relative safety. They've fast-tracked this project. We should have answers in a day or so. Don't go far from your terminals. We may need to call each of you into headquarters for an injection. Alert your mixed blood kin—but only if you are one hundred percent positive they can be trusted. If what we have pans out, it could turn them into valuable allies. Keep the faith. We may prevail."

The screen grayed out. Kate laid a hand over her chest. Her heart pounded.

I'll be damned...

She couldn't believe how quickly Max had gathered a team to storm the lab. She was practically certain he'd acted on the information she gave him.

She walked into the bathroom, cleared the potted flowers she used for a convenient excuse why she hadn't sent her bathtub to the recycling plant, and flipped on the taps. No one at the city would be monitoring water usage tonight. They'd all be too spun out over their lab being pilfered.

She pulled off her top and unbuttoned her jeans. Naked, she caught a glimpse of herself in the mirror. Red welts from Devon's teeth and claws rolled over one shoulder. The corners of her mouth spread into a feral grin. What a hottie. She'd never seen a more sensual shifter. His human and animal forms were damn near perfect—

"I told you. He's our mated one."

"You're relentless. Could you stay out of my thoughts long enough to let me take a bath?"

"No. I'm afraid you'll let him get away."

Kate stepped into the steaming water and, once seated, sank into it. Her shoulder stung when water touched her abraded flesh.

Devon.

She shut her eyes and shook her head, so worried her throat tightened. If things got away from him, and his hands turned into paws, or worse, his face developed a decided feline cast, the other police officers would probably shoot him on the spot.

She slammed her hands on the water's surface. Some sloshed onto the tile floor. Relaxing in the tub had seemed like a good idea, but it wasn't working. She sprang from the water, wrapped a towel around herself, and trotted into the bedroom to check her wrist computer. Maybe he'd texted her, and she hadn't heard it.

"Stop." She spoke out loud. "Just stop. It hasn't even been an hour since he and I spoke."

Her human form chafed. Tonight it felt unnatural, so Kate shifted and sank her claws into the nap of the Oriental rug. She wanted to claw at it, to shred it until nothing was left. Instead, she shook herself from whiskers to tail tip and padded downstairs. Drawing invisibility about herself, she closed two claws around the back door knob and slithered outside. Once she made the forest's edge, she dropped her illusion and ran hard uphill until her flanks heaved and her tongue lolled. When she couldn't run anymore, she raked her claws down a thick aspen trunk.

Kate lay in the debris of the forest floor, panting. At least her emotions were under control. Satisfied she wouldn't make a stupid mistake, she loped toward her house. Near the city streets, she shifted, resurrected invisibility to hide her nakedness, and let herself back inside her kitchen door.

She ran upstairs to check her wrist computer. *Yes!* He'd texted. With nimble fingers that only shook a little she texted him back, grabbed her discarded clothes, and threw them on. She hoped her car started. She hadn't driven it in weeks.

CHAPTER 8

*D*evon set his laser pistol on stun and fired it in a half circle. Things had been a mess when he'd left his patrol car triple parked and waded into the thick of things. With the help of a couple other men from the elite Tracker force, he'd managed to herd the cops into one quadrant. It gave them all a clear shot at the rioters.

Almost as if they understood they were toast, the remaining few hundred demonstrators faded into the night in groups of twos and threes. The only ones left lay prone on the asphalt. Devon wasn't worried about them. The meat wagon could pick them up. Maybe after a few days in a group cell with real criminals, they wouldn't be so quick to sign on for a rebellion. Unless they were shifters, then they'd be dead…

He swallowed hard and glanced surreptitiously at his hands. Thank Christ they looked normal.

"Hey, Heartshorn." A cop he vaguely recognized slugged him in the arm.

"Yeah?" He quirked a brow. "Looks like we're about done here. I'm going home."

"Uh—you got a minute?" The other man, Tanaka, looked

uncomfortable. Shorter than Devon with a bullet-shaped body, his black hair was cut short. Almond eyes and high cheekbones made him look like a sumo wrestler.

Devon's gut tightened. "Sure. But make it snappy. I'm on at zero eight hundred tomorrow morning. It's gonna be a short night."

Tanaka beckoned to him and walked a few paces away. He looked over a shoulder to make certain Devon was following, and then faded into the shadows of an alleyway. Once Devon caught up, he turned off his microphone and gestured for Devon to do the same.

Devon clicked off his mike. "This is against regulations, Tanaka. Whatever it is better be good."

The other man dropped his gaze. "No easy way to say this. You had all those infusions just like me. Have you, ah, noticed anything odd?"

Devon was used to masking his emotions. Good thing too. If Tanaka were a friend, answering might have been a struggle. As things stood, he didn't even blink. "Like what?"

"My hearing's so sharp it gives me a headache. Everything stinks. And I've had dreams…"

Devon dredged up a grin. "The drug was supposed to enhance our sense of smell." He shrugged. "Bet you can smell me since I have some shifter blood. Lots of us do."

Tanaka shook his head. He beckoned for Devon to step closer and spoke in his ear. "I have shifter blood too. Not much, maybe twenty-five percent. There are so many scents, it's confusing. Can't sort them out. It might help if I could sleep… As soon as I drop off, a wolf chases me…"

"Maybe you should drop by the doc's office."

An odd look crossed the other man's face. "Uh, no, can't do that. The department doc would think I'm nuts. If I took another psychological, I'd probably fail. I can't afford to be booted off the force."

"Mmph. I can see where you'd be worried." Devon stepped back a pace. He wanted this conversation to be over. He couldn't help Tanaka without revealing he'd crossed the line and shifted and he wasn't ready to do that.

"Please." The other officer gripped his arm hard. "Don't say anything."

"I won't." Devon stuck out his hand. Tanaka shook it.

"Sorry I bothered you." Tanaka trotted back to the cordoned line and started dismantling it with some other officers.

Devon clicked his mike back on and told Command Central he was leaving. Normally, he'd have asked for permission, but he didn't want to risk them saying no. If they canned him, it would save him the trouble of quitting.

He loped to his car, got in, dragged the black market computer out of the console, and texted Kate. When he didn't hear back from her immediately, he drove up and down side streets until he found an out-of-the way parking spot. While he waited for her to text him back, he thought about Tanaka. The man obviously had a similar reaction to the series of infusions. Lots of people had shifter blood. How many of the elite Tracker force had come into their own as shifters because of the series of treatments?

Devon got out of the car and opened its trunk. He had civilian clothes stashed in it. Better to get out of his uniform and riot gear. People would be less likely to notice him. Dressed in jeans, shirt, and his leather vest, he crawled back into the driver's seat.

He must've drifted off. The computer's squawking woke him. He'd have to scroll through the menus to see if he could come up with a less obnoxious tone.

He glanced at the display. It read, *My office in forty-five minutes. Use the alley door.*

He texted he'd be there and dropped the computer back into the console between the seats. Devon rubbed his temples. Kate's office wasn't far. He'd have time to scare up some coffee. Tired as he was, the thought of seeing her again brought a smile to his face. At least parking shouldn't be a problem at this hour.

He leaned against the wall of a building in Kate's alleyway and waited, foam cup in hand. He'd left his regular wrist computer, microphone, and earpiece in the car, blocks away. The coffee was bitter. It had obviously been a while since it was brewed, but it was better than nothing.

He glanced around the narrow back street. It was clean, which surprised him. Most alleyways overflowed with filth and were filled with homeless people. A single car garage was tucked under Kate's office, right next to the steps he'd come down the previous afternoon. He snorted. Private parking was virtually unobtainable. How had she managed to swing office space that included parking?

Headlights lit the night. He flattened himself against the wall and drew his pistol. It was probably Kate, but he believed in being ready for anything. A silvery electric car slowed. The garage door screeched as it ratcheted upward. Devon holstered his weapon.

The car slid into the garage, and Kate got out. She walked toward him, her heels clicking on asphalt. When she emerged from the garage, the door started to close. Either it was on a timer, or some sort of beam activated it.

"Sorry if you had to wait. I had to plug in to juice up the battery. I don't drive much. Come on." She passed her palm over a recessed pad and the door at the bottom of the staircase clicked open. He trailed after her up carpeted steps.

"How'd you get lucky enough to find an office with a garage?"

"I own the building."

Devon's eyes widened as he stepped through the upper door. She shut it behind him. "It's none of my business," he blurted, "but if you have that kind of money, why work?"

Kate flipped a switch, and the small room behind the bedroom where they'd made love was bathed in pale light. "How about if we go into the front office and sit for a bit?"

"Sure." By the time he got there, she'd drawn the shades.

"I'll leave the lights out. This room is shielded, plus I've added magic. It would take pretty sophisticated surveillance equipment to hear our conversation." She settled into an overstuffed chair and gestured for him to take the one across from it. "The short answer to your question is I bought this building shortly after it was constructed—"

"But it's over a hundred years old."

"A hundred twenty-three to be precise. I actually purchased it a few years before I moved here. Shifters live a long time, so we learn to plan ahead. But that's not what you need me for."

Devon gathered his scattered thoughts. "Right. Shifting. How can I control it?"

She cocked her head to one side, her expression serious. "Nothing like practice. Set down your coffee, stand up, take your clothes off, and visualize yourself as a cat."

"You just want to see me naked."

She nodded. "That too, but I promise I'll keep my hands to myself. This is important. You should have a mountain cat bond mate. Has he tried to talk to you yet?"

"No. Thank God." Devon shinnied out of his vest, jeans, boots, and shirt and imagined himself a cat. Nothing happened. His face heated. He tried again. "Maybe this isn't going to be as big a problem as I thought," he muttered. "If I can't will myself into my other form, it won't get away from me."

She snorted. "Don't be so sure of that." Kate licked her lips. She got to her feet and walked close to him. In a single, fluid motion, she dragged her top over her head. Her lush breasts with their rosy nipples were inches from his chest. His cock stiffened, remembering what it felt like to be inside her. He groaned and cuddled her breasts, teasing them with his fingertips.

She leaned into his hands, her amber gaze never leaving him. Kate trailed her fingers over his erection. "Mmmm... Let's go have some fun with that."

"*Yes!*" Her cat screeched so loud Kate flinched. "*Let's fuck him again and make him ours. Forever. I'll talk with his cat.*"

"*You'll do no such thing.*"

"Are you all right?" Concern underscored his words. "I could've sworn I heard someone else talking about fucking and ours and forever and no such thing."

She nodded. "Just a little discussion with my cat—"

"Your cat talks with you?" Devon pushed against the boundaries of his preconceived notions about how the world worked. It wasn't easy.

"Of course. She obviously wanted to include you in the conversation, or you wouldn't have heard her. Your cat will talk with you too, once you learn to hear his voice. They're wiser than we are in lots of ways." Kate rolled her eyes. "Maybe if you're lucky, yours won't be as opinionated as mine."

"I heard that."

"Be quiet. I agree with you about him, but let me handle this my own way."

Devon quirked a brow. "I see what you mean. She's a bit on the bossy side."

"You don't know the half of it." Kate grinned. "We can talk later, but there's a reason we're so attracted to each other."

"Good. I like reasons." He twirled her nipples until they lengthened into stiff peaks. His cock got even harder. He thrust his hips forward, and she took him in her hands, flicking the tip of his shaft.

"Jesus, that feels amazing, but what about teaching me to shift?"

She shrugged. "Ever heard of playing the ball where it lays? We can always work on shifting. Besides, once you're more relaxed, it will be easier." Kate turned. He followed her swaying hips to the bed. Lust made every nerve ending feel like it was on fire. He couldn't wait to sink inside her. He'd fuck her until both of them couldn't walk.

She slithered out of her jeans and slipped a condom over him. Kate turned away and bent over the bed, feet planted firmly on the floor. The well-formed globes of her ass separated revealing a slick, wet pussy framed by red curls. She didn't need foreplay any more than he did. He wrapped a hand around his erection and guided himself inside her.

As the heat of her body closed around him, he almost lost it and came right then. He'd never been this hot before. His dick was so sensitive it almost hurt. He pulled out and drove himself deep once more. Her ass slammed against his thighs.

Devon placed his hands on her hips and set a rhythm. The harsh sound of their breathing was loud in his ears. He felt himself swell even more. He had to come soon, or—

"It worked," she crowed. "Open your eyes. We're shifting. We'll finish as cats."

He was so lost in lust, it was all he could do to pry his eyes open. Fur covered them both. His vision was strange just like last time. Her scent hammered him. He dropped his body atop hers and closed his mouth over her neck. His cock plumbed her. She drove hard against him, making a wonderful growling sound, which only made him hotter.

Just like last time, the heat of his climax shook him to the end of every nerve ending. Coming as a human wasn't nearly this intense. Her muscles milked him. She screamed, feral and untamed. He rammed her again and again until her body quieted.

Devon started to withdraw, and then hesitated. He didn't want to hurt her. He licked her neck. She arched her back against him and purred.

"It will be all right," she murmured deep in his mind. *"Pull out nice and slow."*

Once he was out of her, he dropped to all fours. She joined him. *"Take time getting used to how this body feels. Walk around a bit. Last time you were so freaked out, you couldn't wait to be human again."*

He padded into the front office, then back to the bedroom. He cleared the bed with a single leap, landing on the other side. Laughter bubbled up. It came out as a growly purr. *"Wow! This is pretty neat."* He leapt over a small table and sidled up next to her.

"Yes, it is. Now think about your human body. Visualize shifting back

into it." Her cat form shimmered as if to demonstrate. In a moment, she was human.

He did the same thing. Devon moved toward her. She shook her head. "No, do it again. Back to cat. Then back to human. Think about how it feels going each way."

After half an hour, she let him stop practicing. He sank onto the bed. Sweat dripped from him. "Not as effortless as you make it look."

Kate grinned. "No, but it really does get easier. Here." She walked to him, bent, and skinned his foreskin back so she could dig the remains of the condom out of its folds. "Shifters don't really need condoms. We decide when we get pregnant. And we're not susceptible to human diseases."

"So why put one on me?" He quirked a brow.

"Because I didn't have time to explain before." She squeezed him lightly. He felt himself harden in her hands.

Devon rolled his eyes. "I don't get it. I haven't been this horny since I was fifteen."

Kate tossed back her head and laughed. "Shifters love sex. We live for it. You asked why I work. I do it to look normal and because it gives me unlimited access to men. Now, if I had a shifter partner —" her gaze locked with his "—I wouldn't need all those other guys."

"Well, why don't you?" His muscles tensed. Her answer was important. He was pretty sure he was falling in love with Kate. The last thing he needed was a woman who ran around. That had been the death knell for his marriage.

"Why don't I what?"

He gestured impatiently. "Have a shifter partner?"

Her hand stopped moving on his shaft. He was fully erect again. Kate looked away and nodded. She seemed engaged in an internal conversation. He didn't want to prod her into answering before she was ready. His cock throbbed. It was tender, but it wanted inside her again.

She let go of him and sat on the bed. "We're animals as much as human," she began. "We can't mate with just anyone." She shoved her hair back over her shoulders, exposing her breasts. Their generous curves and glowing nipples took his breath away. "I'm not explaining this very well. We can have all the sex we want with human partners, but it's only a teaser. It doesn't resonate in here." She tapped her breastbone. "Only shifter sex can do that."

He smiled. "Yes, I understand that loud and clear. But I still don't know why you don't have a shifter partner."

"We don't get to choose. Either your mate shows up—or they don't." Her voice ran down. "Not that we don't, uh, practice with other shifters hunting for the right one. When you live long enough, though, sometimes you just sort of give up. Lots of us end up marrying humans."

Devon digested what she'd told him. Hope speared through him; he batted it aside and cleared his suddenly dry throat. "Does that mean what I think it does...that we're somehow meant for each other? Is that the reason you talked about earlier?"

Her gaze held his, amber eyes alight with something he didn't have a name for. She nodded and held out her arms. He tangled his body with hers. They ended up lying on the bed cradling one another.

Emotions so deep they rocked him to his core filled him: love, protectiveness, tenderness for the woman lying in his arms. Nothing bad would ever happen to her. Not on his watch. His cat, silent until now, purred agreement. It took a while before Devon could talk. "Say more about us being linked. I feel it, but I'm trying to understand."

She nodded and raised her gaze to meet his. "It's not linked. It's mated, though I suppose they mean about the same thing. There were lots of reasons I had a hard time believing it. When you were here earlier, you seemed disgusted with your animal form. Beyond that, there was no way I was tying myself to one of the enemy. But the more I thought about it, the harder it was to deny the attraction between us. I shifted spontaneously when we first made love. That's a dead giveaway. We do that when our mated one shows up.

"My cat had to remind me. I'd forgotten."

She bit her lower lip. Her amber eyes glowed golden. "When I saw you lounging against the alley wall, and all I wanted to do was jump you, wrap my legs around you, and take you inside me, I knew my cat was right. You truly are my mated one." She sucked in a breath. "You've been thinking about me too."

"Obsessed would be more accurate." His face split into a broad grin. He was so happy, his body couldn't contain it. Joy spilled over, casting the room in a numinous glow. "I even jacked off in the shower after I left you. Couldn't figure out why I needed to come again."

She reached between them, cradled his cock, and rolled onto her back so he could slip inside. "Let's stay human this time." Her legs wrapped around him.

"And how will I manage to do that?" Devon stroked her hair back from her face and then balanced himself on his arms, looking down at her. Love for her branded his soul. So did lust, though how he could still even be capable of fucking was beyond him.

Kate's eyes twinkled. "Now you've shifted a few times, you know the feel of your human shape. Keeping your eyes open helps too."

"That part won't be hard. You're gorgeous."

She crinkled her nose. "Bet you say that to all the girls." Her muscles tightened around him. So did her legs. She rocked her pelvis.

Devon drew back and slowly sank inside her again. "You feel so good," he murmured. He wanted to go slow, really slow, so she'd come over and over again. After about twenty long, slow strokes, her face contorted in ecstasy, her nipples peaked, and color suffused her face. Her hands gripped his hips and pulled hard. She ground herself against the base of his cock, and her pussy clenched again and again.

He couldn't tear his gaze away. She was the most perfect, the most amazing creature he'd ever seen. Now that he knew what to look for, the feline cast to her eyes and cheekbones stood out clearly, lending her an exotic look. He inhaled the musk of her arousal. Suddenly he didn't want to wait. His penis jerked deep inside her, taut with need. It wouldn't take very much to bring him to another climax.

Kate gazed up at him and licked her lips suggestively. She jackknifed out from under him, rolled him onto his back, and knelt above him. Her mouth closed over his cock. One hand cradled his balls, the other pumped his shaft. He buried his hands in her magnificent hair and showed her what he needed. An orgasm spooled deep in his belly. His balls tightened, and then he was coming and coming, spasming hard into Kate's magical mouth. His cock was sensitive almost to the point of pain. It intensified his pleasure beyond anything he'd ever experienced. Breath caught in his throat, and his heart thudded against his ribs.

She moved up his body till she lay next to him and kissed him deeply. He tasted himself on her tongue. It got him going all over again. She reached for his still-hard cock, but he pushed her hand away. "You're going to be the death of me." He hugged her. "Besides, I have to go to work. It must be at least seven. Light's filtering in through the drapes."

She kissed him tenderly, then extricated herself and sat cross-legged on the bed looking at him. "Remember what I said about dancing on both sides of the street?"

He nodded somberly and drew his brows drew together. "Your people had something to do with last night's robbery, didn't they? You must've told them about the effect the drug had on me."

Kate looked away. He took one of her hands and stroked it. "I'm in love with you, Kate. Maybe it's the mated one thing, but I've never felt this strongly before about anyone or anything. You have nothing to fear from me. I'd die before I'd hurt you. Or before I'd let anyone else harm you."

She shook her head, not looking at him. "You're still a cop.

You've been one long enough that's where your first allegiance is."

He started to say no, then realized it would take time for him to walk away from a fifteen year career. "I really do plan to quit the force." He laughed bitterly. "Not that I have much choice, but I've been thinking about it for a while now. Came close after Mom died. Probably would have, but I didn't know what else to do. Still don't." He gazed at her intently. "Would you really want me if I was destitute and had no visible means of support?"

"Yes. Except you won't be. You can work for our side. Bet you have a great transferrable skill set."

He chuckled. "That was the right answer. Will you still feel that way after we've made love a thousand times and you're tired of me?"

"I'll never get tired of you." She smiled and winked. "Was that a promise? About a thousand times?"

Devon laughed, wrapped a hand around his cock, and waggled it at her. "If you don't wear him out before then." He let go of himself and slapped his thigh with a hand. "I just had an idea. You obviously have some sort of shifter connections. Tell them one of the other officers on the Tracker task force approached me after the riot. He asked if I'd experienced anything unusual since the infusions."

Kate furled her brows. "Interesting. What did you tell him?"

"Nothing. But it's obvious he's either shifted, or is moving in that direction. There are fifty of us. All the names and birthdates are in a database at the station. If I hack into it and get the list, do you suppose you could find out how many of us had shifter blood to start with?"

She nodded. "Sure. I can do that. Probably within a few hours."

Devon whistled. "You guys are pretty organized."

She snorted. "Only reason we're still alive. Where'd you learn to be a hacker?"

He grinned wryly. "Police academy. They taught me so I could trip up the bad guys. Once I'm in the personnel system, I'll bring the list up on my wrist computer. You can print it. Best not run it through your computer unless you have a secured network."

"I have a secure feed."

"Why am I not surprised? Even better."

"You've got some sort of plan." She bit her lower lip; worry hooded her eyes. "What is it?"

His jaw tightened. "I can do more damage with sabotage from the inside than a direct attack to the outer ranks would accomplish. All successful insurrections have inside people gumming up the works."

He got up and grabbed his wrist computer. His fingers flew over the display. "I can't believe how easy that was." He grinned at her. "The cop shop should've put me in the IT department. There. Just sent the list to your printer. I assume it's the one labeled Kate's Wireless."

She nodded and blew out a worried-sounding breath. "This whole undercover thing is uber dangerous. You'd be safer joining us directly—"

"Not yet. Let me take advantage of what I have. Right now I'm still a trusted member of the force. I'll pay Tanaka a visit before the day's out."

"Who?"

"The officer who approached me. If I can organize a few of us, we could probably take the whole force down—at least for long enough so your people can spring whoever's left in prison. When would be a good time to see you tonight? I can get those names from you then. I'm anticipating there're at least ten of us with new, um, abilities. Maybe more."

"I think you should talk with Max."

"Who's that?"

"The head of the shifter underground in California."

Devon considered it. Coordinated approaches were usually best. "Let me see how many men I can interest in what I have in mind."

"Are you going to tell me what that is?"

He shook his head. "Safer for you if you don't know any details. It's kind of like all those questions rattling around in my head about your organization. Probably safer for both of us if I don't know too much about it yet. What time tonight?"

"How about eight or nine?"

He thought about what Kate had online for the day. Jealousy shot a dart into his tired brain. "Do you have clients?"

She bent to kiss him. "Not sure. If I do, I'll be cancelling them. I'm in love with you too. My head's spinning with it. It's like a part of my soul that was always empty is full, and it feels so damned good I want to screech it to the skies."

"You said that way better than I could have." He bent his head and brushed his lips against hers. "I felt drawn to you from the moment I saw you. I didn't understand why, but you were all I could think about." He cocked his head to one side. "All I wanted to think about."

Kate nodded knowingly. "The mate bond is why it happened so quickly. And why the feelings are so strong. The cat part of me is head over heels. Usually, she's the wise one. My human side overthinks things. There's a lot you don't know about being a shifter. One of them is once we find our mated one, it's forever and we don't share."

He grinned at her. "Does that mean you'll trust me with where your house is? Not that I don't like it here," he waved an arm expansively, "but I'm hoping for dinner and some cuddling."

She took a breath and blew it out. It was apparent trust didn't come easy, even after what had passed between them. Her forehead creased into worried lines. "Make certain you're not followed—"

"I'll use the bus system since they can track where my cruiser is. And I'll leave all the electronics at my house except the wrist computer we've been texting on, which isn't traceable." Emotion swelled within him, thickening his throat. "Kate, I'd lay down my life before I let anything happen to you."

Her eyes welled. She came into his arms and clung to him. "Okay. I'm in the hills. Take the last left after…"

CHAPTER 9

K ate closed the back door behind Devon and activated the lock once she heard the lower door shut. Worry made her nearly ill. She felt warm and vaguely nauseous. She'd had to bite her tongue to keep from begging him not to report for duty. Putting himself square in the path of their enemies just seemed too risky. She walked into the bedroom and culled through her bag for her wrist computer. A few taps brought up her calendar. Only one client today. She hadn't been certain when Devon asked.

Is it too early to call him?

She hustled to the computer in her front office and brought up the client's personal data. He preferred to be texted. Great. That made things easy. She hesitated, her fingers hovering over the keys. If she made a blanket announcement that she was closing her practice, it would be sure to arouse suspicion. Nope, probably better to say she'd caught some sort of bug and would call when she felt better.

Once she'd cleared the rest of her week of clients via a combination of texting and voice mails, Kate printed Devon's list and tapped into the scrambled frequency for the underground.

Max shimmered into life on her screen. "Up early, aren't you, Miss Roman?"

"Not really. But I am at my office early. Mostly because I spent the night here. There are some things you need to know. And something I need too…" She launched into an abbreviated account of Devon's plans—what little she knew of them—and asked if she could scan and upload the list of names.

Max tugged at an earlobe. His face scrunched into a frown. "Do you know how to get hold of Devon?"

Kate's face heated. She wished the vid feed weren't in color.

"Oh ho, so it's like that, is it? What, he got pretty hot after he shifted?"

She shook her head. "I know better. He's my mated one. I tried to ignore it, but all the signs fit. For him too. It's why I'm so worried. I've been alone forever. Now that I've found him, I don't want to lose him."

Max's joking demeanor fell away. "Did you tell him he should join us?"

"Yes."

"And?"

"He's got some harebrained scheme to gather all the Tracker task force who've morphed into shifters and talk them into sabotaging the police department. He thinks it'll work because they'll all understand at a bone-deep level that they're seriously screwed."

Max steepled his fingers and rested his chin on them. "That could work—but only on a large scale. It would need to be done here—and all across the nation—at precisely the same time for maximum effect. I shouldn't tell you this, Roman, but we've had a few hours to analyze the serum. Didn't take our crew long. They're all competent Ph.Ds.

"You told me Devon had gotten half a dozen infusions." He glanced at her for corroboration. When she nodded, he went on. "Turns out one would have done it. Like everything the government gets their paws into, they fucked this one up too."

Kate drew back. Her heartbeat sounded loud in her ears. "What exactly does that mean? Will it kill him?"

"No. But it will amp his ability to use our magic to the nth degree. His buddies too. Turns out even ten percent shifter blood will respond to the drug. We staged raids on every lab in the state once we were sure. We've begun gathering those with mixed blood and giving them the serum. By this time next week, our ranks will have swelled by several hundred percent."

Excitement thrummed through her. "What then?"

"Once we have a critical mass, we'll take the bastards on." Max's normally laconic expression turned wolfish as he let his animal side show through. "Your Tracker task force angle is one I hadn't thought of. I'll alert my contacts throughout the country. Those elite task force guys are trained death machines. We'll need to give any of them who sign on with us a crash course in how to focus their magic."

Kate fell back against her chair, stunned. "How much of this can I tell Devon?"

"If he's your mated one, he can read your mind."

She shook her head. "He doesn't know how to manipulate his magic yet—"

Max tossed back his head and hooted with laughter. "Well, Miss Roman, maybe you should stay out of bed long enough to teach him." After a few more wolfish snorts, he added, "On a more serious note, once we find out which of his Tracker group has shifter blood, we'll gather the willing ones to entrain their magic. Caution him not to do anything ahead of time that might give our plans away. No Rambo stunts."

She thought about Devon's initial reaction to shifting. "Er, what if some of the Tracker task force don't want to be shifters?"

Another snort of mirth. "None of them will want to be shifters, but they're grown men. They'll understand they're stuck between a rock and a dagger. Besides—" he grinned, showing long incisors "—once they get to know us, they'll like us. We do tend to grow on people. Nothing quite like tapping into the inner beast, eh? Near immortality has quite the appeal too. Got to run, Roman. You just gave me more to do. Upload that list. I'll shoot it back to you once I have answers. Oh, yes. Stop by one of our clinics. We're giving small amounts of the serum to everyone."

Kate scanned the list and sent it on its way. She tried to wrap her mind around the implications of what Max had told her. A nationwide uprising. If they were successful, it would be like turning back the clock. Shifters could walk in daylight again without hiding what they were.

Her stomach rumbled. She hadn't had much to eat the previous day. Kate looked down at herself and grinned. Still naked. She sniffed. Devon's scent—spicy and exotic—made her nostrils quiver. She ran a hand down her body, wishing it was his fingertips caressing her, and then forced herself to get moving.

She showered, dressed, and set the locks. The only thing left was waiting to hear back from Max. She checked her terminal again. The LED blinked red. She booted up and printed the list. Too dangerous to transfer it to her wrist computer. Maybe she should stop and get a black market one like Devon's, except she didn't have the first idea where she could find something like that.

She scanned the list, and her eyes widened. Out of fifty names, forty-three of them had enough shifter blood for the infusion to kick them over the edge. Forty-two, plus Devon. She wanted to text him. His wrist computer was safe, but hers wasn't. It would have to wait. She wished they'd made plans to meet for lunch.

Kate snapped her fingers. Just because they hadn't set up a midday date didn't mean it was too late. She texted him using his regular wrist computer. He'd given her that number too.

He texted back immediately with an address not far from her. Kate hurried out the door. It was early for lunch, but the raw need to see him heated her blood. She decided to walk to the café. It was only about half a mile. Maybe by the time she got there, she'd have herself under better control. Besides, even if she drove, there wouldn't be any place to park. She loved her electric car. Roomy ones like hers were nearly impossible to find nowadays. The new ones were so small, they'd barely accommodate two adults. Children and pets were out of the question.

She settled into an easy, loping stride. The city looked different today, less like a prison. For the first time in a long time, she felt hopeful—about a lot of things.

~

Kate sat next to Devon on a small bench. They were just finishing lunch. She could've sat across the rickety, metal table, but she'd wanted to feel him next to her. Plus, this way she'd been able to whisper to him. Once she made certain he'd left all his electronic toys in his car, she'd relayed everything Max told her about the infusions.

"We have a few minutes before you have to get back. Tell me about yourself," she murmured. "I want to know everything."

He shrugged. "It's pretty simple, really. I grew up in San Bernardino. Two sisters. Dad's still alive. You already know what happened to Mom. I graduated from UCLA and signed on with the San Bernardino Sheriff's Department. I thought I could save enough money for law school, but I made the mistake of getting married—"

"Married?" Kate drew back. "What happened to her?"

He blew out a breath. "It was more what happened to us. I wasn't home much. She took up with other men. We went our separate ways a whole lot of years ago."

"Girlfriends since then?"

He grinned at her. "Why? Are you feeling jealous?"

"Maybe a little."

"Nah, I've pretty much kept to himself. Not that there haven't been women, but none of them ever meant anything to me."

She cuddled closer and wrapped a hand around his forearm. "I'm glad."

"Your turn." He laid a hand over hers.

"Um, I was born in what's now New York."

He furled his brows. "How long ago?" She bent close and whispered. A long, low whistle escaped him.

"Stop that. People will look at us."

"They already are—" merriment danced behind his dark eyes "—because we've been pawing at one another like a couple of randy kids."

Kate straightened and moved so a few inches separated them. "There. Is that better?"

"No." He draped an arm around her and pulled her against his body. "Are your parents alive?" She nodded. "Where?"

"They're still on the east coast. I have a sister and brother too, one older, one younger."

"How long since you've seen them?"

"Not since before," she leaned close, "the, um, problems with our kind. We do talk, though. Maybe a couple times a month."

"College?"

Kate snorted. "I went to a one-room school. College came a long time later. When I was young, women weren't allowed to go."

"Husbands?"

"Why?" She mimicked his grin from earlier. "Jealous?"

"You bet!"

A warm place bloomed in her heart. She wanted Devon to care who she'd been with. "No husbands. You'll be the first."

He laughed, and then clapped a hand over his mouth. "Not that I'm opposed to the idea, but—"

"You thought I'd sit back demurely and wait for you to do the asking?"

Color stained his bronze skin, giving it a rosy cast. "Something like that." He cocked his head to one side. "Say, I'd really like to hear what it was like when you were, er, young. Bet you have an interesting slant on history."

Kate glanced around the restaurant. There were a few too many people for her to feel comfortable saying much more. "I'll tell you when we're alone." She nuzzled his neck. "I love you. I still can't get over that we found each other."

"Aw, darling." He bent and pressed his lips lightly over hers. "I feel the same way."

Deep within, her cat purred extravagantly. *I found him for us.*

So you did. Just don't say I told you so.

Devon drained his coffee and picked at some scraps of sandwich left on his plate. "On a more serious note..."

He was just beginning to question her more closely about Max when his wrist computer vibrated. She glanced at the screen. *Incoming Call* flashed in red. She quirked a brow.

"Means it's one of the task force. I need to take it." He tapped a couple keys. "Heartshorn."

Kate leaned close to listen.

"Detective?" a female voice with a strong Asian accent asked.

"Actually, I'm a lieutenant. Who is this?"

"I am Ray Tanaka's wife. Please, I do not know who to call. He seemed to like you—"

"Seemed? Did, ah, something happen to him?" Devon's features developed a strained aspect.

"Yes. Please. If you could come to our house."

Kate tapped Devon's arm, nodding furiously.

"Sure," Devon said. "Run the address by me." He clicked the end call icon and addressed his next words to Kate. "Done eating?"

"Yeah." She folded her napkin and laid it on the table. "Let's go."

"Do you have your car?"

"No. Can't we take yours?"

The skin around his eyes pinched in worry. "No. We're not supposed to transport civilians unless it's an emergency, plus the department has a tracking device in every police car. Even though I hate to add half an hour, we need to go back and get yours. Last thing we need is another officer nosing around."

She set off at a jog. He paced her. "If this is what I think it is—" he began.

"Pretty much has to be," she broke in. "He's in his—" she glanced around to see if anyone was close enough to overhear "—um, other form and can't get back. His wife's probably terrified."

"Can you help?"

"Of course, unless he's so far gone he won't listen to me."

Devon gripped her hand as they ran. "What then?"

Kate thought about what Max had said about the Tracker elite being trained death machines. She frowned. "Not sure. I'd need to call Max."

They ran around her building and up the alley. She activated the electronics from her wrist computer; the garage door slid open. "I'll drive," she said. "Could you program the address into the online database?"

His fingers flew over the display while she backed out. "Ready?" he asked. She nodded, and he tapped the *Find It* icon. The car edged out of the alley and took a left turn. It would get them to the address in its automotive brain without any assistance.

"Is there somewhere I can read more about the things I need to know about being a shifter? What if you hadn't been sitting right next to me? I'd have gone to Tanaka's house and been clueless."

"We've never written things like that down."

"But how can I learn if there're no materials to study?" he persisted.

"According to Max, once we get all forty-three of you rounded up and flying the same direction, he's going to chuck the lot of you into a crash course in magic."

"Car's slowing down."

She glanced through the windshield at a well-kept, but older neighborhood with bungalow-style homes. Kate disconnected the autopilot and looked for a parking spot. "That's the address, isn't it?" He nodded. "Do you suppose they'd mind if I parked in their driveway?"

"Don't see why not."

The car doors opened. Once she and Devon cleared the electronic beam, they swooshed shut and locked. Devon moved ahead of Kate. "Let me go first, in case there's something we hadn't anticipated."

She dropped behind him. It felt good to be side-by-side with Devon. They fit together—mentally and physically. A pleasant vibration hummed between them. If she'd been in her cat form, she would've purred. It had been hard to keep her hands off him during lunch. Not that she'd done all that good a job.

He raised his hand to knock, but the door opened before he could. A diminutive Asian woman with waist-length dark hair and huge dark eyes peered out the door. "Who's she?" The woman pointed at Kate.

"It's okay, Mrs. Tanaka. She's a friend of mine. I had a feeling I knew what might be wrong. I brought her along to help."

The woman's face crumpled. "I am Makiko. Please to come in."

Kate heard the click of several deadbolts as the woman locked the door behind them.

An ominous growl came from the back of the house. Coyote? She sniffed the air. No, wolf. Kate sucked in a breath and took a chance. She walked to the woman. "Makiko. Your husband has taken another form. Am I correct?"

The woman's eyes widened. She drew back. "H-how could you possibly know that? W-what are you?"

"It's the injections," Devon said. "The ones for the task force. Ray had shifter blood, and the drug made it strong enough for him to shift."

Makiko sank onto a footstool and dropped her head into her hands. "I thought maybe it was something like that." She raised her gaze to Devon, pleading in her eyes. "Can you make him human again?"

"Yes—" Devon began.

"Maybe," Kate said firmly. "Where is he?"

"Right behind you."

A low growl spun Kate around. She made a split second decision, shucked her clothes, and reached for her cat form. She circled him, her tail swishing. *"You're still thinking in words. That's a good sign. A very good sign. Did you see me shift?"*

"Yes. What does that have to do with...? Holy shit, is that what happened? I've turned into one of them?" The large, gray timber wolf fell onto his haunches, threw back his muzzle, and howled.

"Stop, stop." Makiko held out her hands. "We have neighbors. They'll turn us in."

"Get hold of yourself." Kate made her mind voice stern. *"Right now."* She gathered her rear legs under her, ready to spring and bite him if she had to.

Tanaka quieted. His amber eyes held a haunted cast. He got all four feet under him and paced up and down the smallish living room. *"You went from woman to cat. How can I reverse the process?"*

"Quiet your mind. Visualize your human form. It will come."

He barked once. It sounded like the human equivalent of "ha" to her.

"Look." Kate shimmered back to her human form. "It's easy. The reason you feel trapped is because you're upset. When we're upset, we can't shift. Come on, Ray. Take a few breaths. Calm yourself and reach for your human form." She picked up her clothes and dressed, never taking her gaze from him.

Devon came up behind her and placed his hands on her shoulders. "Do you think—?"

"Ssht. Let's give him a chance." The air around Tanaka took on a luminous glow. *"You're on the right track,"* Kate murmured in mind speech. *"Just keep doing what you're doing."*

The air quieted, and then glowed again. On Tanaka's fourth try, the wolf disappeared. Tanaka's human eyes were wide with horror; his mouth opened and closed like a landed fish. He glanced down. His hands dove to his crotch to cover himself, and he skittered out of the room with Makiko right behind him.

A door slammed shut.

Devon dropped his mouth next to Kate's ear. "Well played. I didn't think he'd be able to find his way back."

"Neither did I," she whispered back.

A few moments passed. Kate heard the low murmur of voices from the room Ray and his wife had disappeared into. "They need to come back out here. We have to talk with them."

"I agree." Devon strode to the closed door and knocked. When no one said anything, he knocked louder, following it with, "Look, man, I know how you feel, but I have to talk with you."

Footsteps sounded. The door cracked open a few inches. "Thank your, ah, friend for me, Heartshorn. I don't feel much like talking. Makiko, she was only trying to help, but she shouldn't have called you."

The door started to shut. Devon jammed his boot between it and the frame. "Put on some clothes, goddamn it, and come out here."

"Give me a minute."

Devon backtracked to Kate. They stood near the front door, waiting. The sound of a knob turning made Kate look up. Danger so thick she could barely breathe flooded her cat senses. She pounded her shoulder into Devon. "Get down," she shrieked. They both hit the floor.

He rolled on top of her and drew his laser pistol. The *phut-phut* of a laser slammed into the front door just behind where they'd been standing seconds before. Kate peered from under Devon and eyed Tanaka. The man held an identical weapon trained right on them.

"Drop it or I'll shoot," Devon said.

"Your girlfriend, abomination that she is, would be dead before you got me."

"What the fuck?" Devon snarled. "She wasn't an abomination when she helped you find your way back."

Makiko burst out of the back room and threw her body between her husband and Devon and Kate. "Go," she screeched. "Just go. He won't shoot me."

Unfolding his body, Devon stood, his gun still trained on Tanaka. "Kate. Get up. Back toward the door. Open it nice and easy."

"But we need to talk with him," she protested, scrambling to her feet. She locked her gaze onto Tanaka's. "What if you shift again? You need to learn how to—"

The gun wavered in his hand. He dropped it to his side. "I don't want to learn anything about being a shifter. Nothing. Not now. Not ever. Please leave. I-I can't believe this happened to me." A sob tore out of him, followed by another. His shoulders heaved. Makiko turned and put her arms around her husband, crooning in Japanese.

Devon backed toward her. "Open the door. We're leaving."

"But—"

"We'll talk about this outside."

Something in his tone got her attention. She reached behind her until she felt the latch, engaged it, and slid out the door. Devon joined her on the porch and eased the door shut. He put a hand on her shoulder and propelled her toward the car.

Before they got to it, she heard the report of a laser pistol and a high, keening cry. She heard the gun again, then silence.

"Was that what I thought it was?" She felt ill. Kate ducked from beneath his arm, spun, and ran for the house.

Devon grabbed her arm and dragged her toward the driveway. "Yes. We need to be gone from here. Now. Unlock your car."

Something about his tone galvanized her into compliance.

They were halfway back to her office before it dawned on her. "You knew."

He nodded. "I speak some Japanese. They took the honorable way out—at least by their code."

Tears pricked behind her lids. One spilled over. "To think we're so hated—" she choked out "—that death is preferable…" Her voice ran down. She swallowed back bile burning the back of her throat. "I could have helped him."

"He didn't want your help. Not mine, either." Devon's ragged breathing rattled against the silence inside the car. "I wonder how the other forty-one of us will fare."

"Crap. I hadn't even thought about that. You did all right—"

"Not at first I didn't. Remember?" He took one of her hands in his. "I had you. It made a hell of a difference."

"Do you want me to drop you at your car?"

"No." His jaw was set in a hard line. "I'd like to come upstairs with you. I'm ready to talk with Max. We need some sort of plan so we don't lose any more potential allies to suicide."

CHAPTER 10

Devon kept an arm around Kate as she guided the car into her garage. She was visibly shaken by what had happened. His heart ached for her, but he didn't know how to soften her pain. He'd seen so much death, he'd found places to pigeonhole it. Ray Tanaka couldn't live with what he'd become, so he checked out. Devon could accept that. Makiko hadn't wished to live with the shame of her husband's dual nature, so she'd followed him into death. In Japanese culture, their deaths were honorable.

He followed Kate up the stairs. Once they got inside, he drew her against him and held her until her tears slowed. "I love you, Kate. If there was some way I could reach into your heart and make you stop hurting—"

"Thanks." She snuffled. "I'm sad, but I'm angry too. He was such a beautiful wolf. What a waste of talent and ability." She tilted her head back until her gaze met his, amber eyes red-rimmed and swollen. "Because he died in human form, the wolf will be lost, wandering endlessly, hunting for his human half. It's just so sad. Being a shifter is a great gift. Tanaka spat on it and cast it aside."

"When we die, it's as animals?" Devon wanted to know more about the cat part of himself.

She nodded. "Yes, our spirits rest easy that way. The animals live forever, and it frees them to find another bond partner."

He led her through the bedroom to the outer office, sat on a plush floral sofa, and drew her against his body. "Tell me some things about being a shifter."

"What would you like to know?"

"How do the human and animal parts integrate?"

She cuddled closer to him and drew her feet up onto the couch. "All I can tell you is how it works for me, but I think it's similar for the rest of us. My human side has one set of feelings and thoughts, my cat side another. The cat is more instinctual, the human more rational. Each side has the utmost respect for her sister."

She took a breath. "When I'm human, the cat lives inside me. When I'm a cat, the human lives inside. For me to kill myself in human form would be the ultimate *fuck you* to my cat. I'd deserve to rot in hell."

"How do you find out which animal is yours? It can't be genetic. Mother was a bear. One aunt is a coyote; another is a wolf. Grandmother is a mountain lion."

"You won't believe it if I tell you."

"Try me." He tightened his arms around her. God, she felt good. Like she belonged next to him—now and always. He kissed her forehead.

Kate wriggled away so she could look at him. "Maybe you will believe me. After all, it's part of your Native American background. Dreaming is, anyway. The animals are immortal. They exist in something like a parallel universe. We dream who our animal will be. We dream them, and they become part of us." She stopped, her forehead furrowed in thought. "Maybe it didn't work that way for you since you were so old when your first shift happened."

Devon pinched the bridge of his nose between his thumb and forefinger. A chill ran down his back. The same one he felt whenever he faced something eerie. "I did have mountain lion dreams. Lots of them from when I was a child until I was, maybe, twenty or so."

Her eyes lit with delight. "See! It was your cat trying to connect, except your blood wasn't strong enough. As soon as it was—"

He laughed. It bubbled up from his belly and filled him with a sense of well-being. "My blood had a hell of a boot in the ass from your considerable charms."

She smiled and shrugged. "Maybe so, but still..." Her smile grew broader. "I'd say that's one happy cat. He waited a long time for you."

"What would have happened if I'd never had those infusions?"

Her face grew serious. "He would have wandered on the other side, waiting. Sort of like Tanaka's wolf is doing right now. Except the wolf knows Tanaka is dead, so he is grieving—and probably furious because he's trapped. Your cat wouldn't have given up until he was certain you were dead."

"And then?"

"Because you had never actually bonded, he would've opened himself to another's dreams. We die in animal form because it frees both human and animal to move forward to whatever comes next."

"The night he tried to talk with me, Tanaka told me he'd had wolf dreams." Devon frowned. "If I'd known more then—" Guilt jabbed him, and he looked away from Kate's forthright gaze.

She stroked his cheek. "Don't blame yourself. You still couldn't have told him anything without compromising yourself."

"Probably so. Animals are amazing, aren't they? Loyal, true, honorable, courageous."

Kate nodded. "All those things and more. I can't imagine not being a shifter. It's added so much richness to my life."

"And I can't imagine a life without you." He pulled her close and kissed her. She fit perfectly against his body. She opened her mouth under his, but he broke away. "I have to go back to work. They'll be trying to raise me on the radio, especially once they find out about Tanaka."

"Do you still want to talk with Max?"

"Yeah, I do."

She looked thoughtful. "Okay, I'll see if I can connect with him through the vid feed, but you go wait in the bedroom until I call you. I need to make certain he wants to talk with you before I blow his identity."

Devon hopped off the couch and walked into the bedroom. Since he had a few moments, he gathered his hair and braided it to get it out of the way. He heard the click of keys and the muted rise and fall of voices. It wasn't long before she called, "Come on. It's okay."

Devon walked briskly to her side and hunkered so he could look at the screen. He whistled, then clapped a hand over his mouth. "Sorry, sir. I wasn't expecting the California state governor."

Max laughed. "No, son, I'll bet you weren't. Miss Roman told me what happened to Tanaka. Damned shame. Predictable, though, when someone turns into what they've been taught to hate. Quite a shock to the system."

"What can we do to make certain the same thing doesn't happen to the forty-one others in the Tracker task force?" Devon asked. "Not to mention others like us in different cities and states."

Max's lips formed a thin, hard line. "Unfortunately, there's not much we can do to keep desperate men and women who've lived by the gun from turning their weapons against themselves."

"What if we warned them?" Kate asked.

Devon spread his hands in front of him. "What would we say? Congratulations, you just won the kewpie doll? You're now a shifter. Most of them would react just like Tanaka. Or like I did, for that fact, until I pulled my head out of my ass. Uh, sorry, sir." He glanced at Max.

"No offense taken. Miss Roman is right that forewarning—or even a frank discussion—might go a long way toward making the news more palatable."

Max frowned. "How about this?" He moved his gaze to Devon.

"Pay your commanding officer a visit. Tell him Tanaka tried to talk with you at the riot. Look uncomfortable, then confide you've had some of the same problems with enhanced hearing and smell, but because you had the whole Native American mystic gig going, you've been able to manage things—"

"That will bring him to their attention and put him at risk," Kate protested.

Devon held up a hand. "Let's hear him out. So far what he's said seems logical. I'm concerned about Tanaka's death. Don't want anyone else doing the same thing. Suicide's quite common among cops. We don't talk much about it, but it bothers all of us."

"Exactly," Max said. "Offer to spend time one-on-one with the other officers, especially the ones with shifter blood. You can even voice a suspicion that maybe the infusion strengthens shifter proclivities—but only a little. Since they have you pegged at twenty-five percent, you have a long way to go before you hit the magic halfway point that would spell your destruction."

"I like it." Devon ran the plan through his head, looking for holes. "It seems like a really clean way to give me access to the rest of the task force. I can feel them out to see who might be a candidate to join us."

Max inclined his head. "Smart man. You understand how powerful this could be." He shifted his gaze to Kate. "Looks like you picked a good one, Miss Roman."

"I still don't like it," she muttered.

Devon took her hand. "None of us will be safe until this is over. I can take care of myself. I've been doing it for a long time."

"Speaking of over." Kate looked at Max. "How long?"

"Not more than a couple of weeks. Hopefully, more like ten days. We can move fast when we need to."

"Sooner is better." Devon creased his brow into a frown. "Someone will blab and jeopardize everything."

"Yes, that's bound to happen," Max agreed. He pointed a finger at Devon. "Watch your back. Best if you simply sound out the other task force members without revealing anything. Work through Miss Roman if you need me." The screen faded to gray.

Devon pushed to his feet and shook his legs to get the kinks out of them from staying in a crouch so long. "I'll be damned," he muttered. "Guess it helps to have friends in high places."

Kate stood and walked in front of him. Her amber eyes were pinched with worry. "Don't delude yourself. If you get into trouble, he can't bail you out without compromising himself."

Devon opened his arms. She stepped into them and wrapped hers around him. Her breasts pressed into his chest. He dropped his hands to her wonderful ass and pulled her against him. Heat roared through him when he kissed her. Her scent eddied in the air, tempting him. His cock strained against his pants. It knew what it wanted: Kate. Any part of her would do.

He broke the kiss. "Kate. My heart, my life. I love you. I don't want to leave your side. Not ever, but I have to go back to work. I'll end up on the defensive if they have to hunt me down."

Her face was flushed, lips slightly parted. "I don't want you to leave, either. I love you, and I'm worried sick something hideous will happen." She gripped his face between her hands. "Maybe you could call in sick. Anything so you didn't have to put yourself at risk."

Devon laid his hands over hers, bent, and kissed the tip of her nose. "If it weren't for Tanaka, I could. Whenever things like this happen, they circle the wagons. They'll be searching for me soon, if they aren't already."

"Oh." She looked distraught, her lips pressed into a worried line. "You have the list of names. You're still coming by later tonight, aren't you?" She dropped her hands to her sides and took a step backward. Tears glistened in her eyes.

His heart swelled. He wanted Kate to love him and want him and miss him when he wasn't by her side. "Of course I'm coming to see you. This isn't any easier for me than it is for you. If I had my way, I'd never leave you again—ever. Here." He dug the list out of a pocket, scanned it, and handed it back to her. "Probably ought to burn this."

"I thought you needed it."

"I do, but I have an eidetic memory. All I needed was to see it."

"If I text or call you, which wrist computer?"

"It would be safer to use the untraceable one. I'm hoping no one saw us at Tanaka's house today. It would be hard to explain."

She twisted her hands in front of her and nibbled her lower lip. "Maybe not all that difficult. You came to me through your doctor. We hit it off and started dating. It's not like I'm a therapist. Surrogates sometimes pair up with men who started out as clients."

"Good to know. Hope I don't have to use the information. Bye, Kate. I love you, sweetheart." His heart swelled. The words tasted sweet on his tongue.

She brushed a hand over his still-erect cock. "Love you too, my mated one. Save some of that for later."

"Mated one. I like the sound of that. So does my cat."

"Oh?" She quirked a brow. "He's started talking already?"

"Mostly, he just purrs, but yes." Devon laughed and let himself out her front door. He felt buoyant inside, light and happy. It was the first time in a long time he'd had something to look forward to. He couldn't wait to gather Kate into his arms later that night, strip her clothes off, and sink deep inside her.

Human sex or cat? Aw, what the hell. We'll do it all.

"Yes." His cat purred agreement. *"She is our mated one. We will love her and care for her forever."*

He sprinted for his car, got in, and collected his wrist computer. Devon groaned when he looked at the display. He tapped keys to listen to seven messages from headquarters, all of them marked urgent. He hit redial on the last one from his captain.

"It's about time, Heartshorn," the captain growled. "Where the fuck have you been?"

"Chasing down leads in plainclothes."

"Humph. Did you listen to all your voicemails?"

"Yes, sir."

"So you know Tanaka killed his wife, then offed himself."

"Yes, sir. I'm sorry, sir."

"I need you at headquarters as soon as you can get here. We're holding a debriefing at sixteen hundred hours."

Devon glanced at the time on his wrist computer. "I can be there in about ten minutes. Could I meet with you before the meeting?"

"About what?"

"I'd rather tell you when I get there, sir."

"Fine." The line went dead.

Devon snorted. His captain certainly wouldn't win any awards for his social abilities, but he was a hell of a good cop. In the brief time Devon had worked for him, he'd developed a solid respect for Captain Lance Aaron.

As usual, the building elevator was on the fritz. Devon took the stairs two and three at a time. He was breathing hard when he made it to the fifth floor where the brass had their offices. He knocked on Captain Aaron's door.

"Come."

His boss looked even more out of sorts than usual. Tall and well-muscled, his brown hair was clipped short. Sharp green gaze zeroed in on Devon. "Sit." He pointed to a chair. Devon dropped into it.

"Got a call after yours. Seems Tanaka had some nosy neighbors. They uploaded a video from right around the time forensics thinks he died. You were in it. Kate Roman was with you. What's up with that? Did you know her before I assigned you to follow her? Spill it, Heartshorn."

Truth had always been Devon's friend. It was possible they'd hook him up to a full-body lie detector, so whatever story he came up with had to be close enough his physical reactions wouldn't give him away.

He sucked in a breath and looked right into Captain Aaron's green eyes. "I'll get to Kate. Let me tell this in order. Tanaka approached me after the riot the other night. He'd been having some, uh, unusual experiences and—"

"What kind of unusual experiences?"

"His senses were so acute they bothered him, and he mentioned dreams where a wolf was chasing him."

"What'd he want from you?" Aaron narrowed his eyes to suspicious slits.

"Since I'd had the same series of infusions, he wanted to know if I'd experienced any of the same things."

His boss leaned forward. "Have you?"

Devon shook his head. "Not really. Nothing I couldn't deal with, anyway."

"Okay, so that was last night. What happened today? How'd you end up at Tanaka's house?"

"That's easy. His wife called me. You can check my wrist computer. She called me from his. I figured it was task force business, so I picked up. She sounded distraught and asked if I could come over."

"Where does Kate Roman fit into this?"

Devon felt heat rise to his face. "Uh, see I was having some problems, and the doctor gave me a referral to her quite a while back. Weeks before she became my assignment. We sort of hit it off, and—"

The captain waved him to silence. "I don't want to know about your sex life. I finally comprehend why you didn't want to implicate her as a shifter, though." He shot Devon a lascivious, knowing look. "I can understand why you'd want to fuck her. She's a pretty hot property, but why'd you drag her to Tanaka's? And why the hell didn't you 'fess up about knowing her? I'd have assigned another officer to check on her."

Devon shrugged. His face got even warmer. It was a struggle not to launch himself across the desk and wind his hands around the captain's neck. "I didn't 'fess up because it's demeaning to tell my captain I needed to see a surrogate." He sucked in a tense breath, managing to look sheepish. "In terms of how Kate factored in, we were eating lunch when the call came in. I thought maybe another woman might be useful calming Tanaka's wife. Kate was game, so we took her car."

"Why didn't you call headquarters?"

Devon shot him an incredulous look. "About a hysterical wife? Come on, Captain. I try not to kick things upstairs until I'm sure there's really a problem."

"Humph. What happened at Tanaka's house?"

"Kate talked to the wife. I talked with him. They both seemed better. He stopped waving his gun around, and we left."

"You didn't see him kill himself? Or his wife."

"No."

Thank Christ he'd had the foresight to get Kate and himself out of there. No matter how capable a forensics team was, there was no way to tie a death to the exact second it happened.

"Was that what you wanted to see me about?"

"Yes, sir, and one other thing—"

"What? Hurry it up. Debriefing's in just a few minutes."

"You've seen my records. I had special psychological training from the San Bernardino County Sheriff's Office. I've noticed a few alterations in how I see the world since I got that series of infusions. I was going to offer to sit down with the guys, sort of one-on-one like, to talk with them." He cleared his throat and studied the floor. "Don't want to lose anyone else, sir."

"I'll think about it and let you know." He stared hard at Devon. "I am not pleased you took a suspected shifter anywhere. You haven't heard the last of this. Dismissed."

Devon opened his mouth to protest Kate wasn't a shifter, but didn't want any more of a confrontation with his boss than he'd already had. He shot to his feet, nodded smartly, and walked out into the hall. He headed for the vending machines to get coffee before the meeting. His head felt fuzzy, not conducive to choreographing his next move. Caffeine might help. Then and again, it might not. His lids were heavy, his muscles sluggish.

"Heartshorn."

Devon spun to face his captain. "Sir?"

"Back in my office."

Devon followed him. His heart beat hard against his ribs. His throat was dry.

Captain Aaron slammed the door. "I just watched the video carefully. You and Roman were in the driveway when shots sounded from inside the house. She made a dash for the door. You dragged her back and stuffed her in the car. Let's play this one again from the top, Heartshorn. By God, if I'm not convinced you've told me everything, I'll hook your sorry ass up to the polygraph."

Devon shrugged. "Fine. I don't quite get the problem, though. I told you I didn't see Tanaka kill himself or his wife, and the video just corroborated it—"

"Shut up and sit down. Once your ass is in the seat, tell me why you hustled Roman out of there."

Kate paced back and forth in her living room. It was nearly ten o'clock with no sign of Devon. Worry made her stomach burn. She'd had a bad feeling when he left her office in the middle of the afternoon, but she'd chalked it up to nerves. She kicked herself for not teaching him how to communicate with her telepathically.

Yeah, right. When would I have had time for that?

When I was rolling around in bed fucking him, her pragmatic side answered.

She glanced at her wrist computer for the umpteenth time. Something flashed across the tiny display. If she hadn't been looking right at it, she would have missed the one frantic word.

Run.

She stared at the screen, but it was blank. She clicked icons. The computer told her an incoming message had aborted. Caller ID listed the originating computer as *Unidentifiable*.

Her eyes rolled frantically. Terror tightened her throat until it was hard to breathe. She grabbed a bag she always kept packed and started down the stairs. Was it safe to take her car, or had it been compromised earlier at the Tanaka house? She wanted to call Max, but that didn't feel safe, either. If they ransacked her house, they might be able to trace the vid feed from her computer. How safe were the scrambled feeds anyway?

Because she wasn't sure, Kate stopped by the terminal and clicked keys frantically. When she was done, the hard drive would self-destruct. If this was a false alarm and she ended up back home, she'd have to buy a new central processing unit.

Kate took a moment and allowed her gaze to linger around her home and her beloved possessions. She clenched her jaws together. They were only things. She could start over just like she'd done lots of times before. The thing she couldn't replace was Devon. He was in big trouble. Had to be. Maybe he was dead...

Stop! If he moved beyond this plane, I'd know.

But would she? Were her thoughts nothing but a panacea to allow her to keep moving?

If she let herself dwell on losing her mated one, she might not care enough about living to give whoever was after her the slip.

In the garage, she made a decision and unplugged the electric motorcycle from its charger. She slipped a helmet over her head and strapped her suitcase to the small luggage rack. Her car stuck out like a sore thumb, especially if the police were looking for her. The bike would blend right in. She knotted her hair and tucked it under her jacket. Without it to give her away, she could pass for either sex, at least from a distance.

She fanned magic about her and listened intently with her cat senses. Nothing. Kate didn't hesitate. She backed the bike out of the garage, punched the button to lower and lock the door, and raced down the street. She hadn't gone two blocks before she heard the distant thrum of engines.

Vehicles, heading her way.

Her eyes raked the darkness. She didn't want to meet whoever was coming up the warren of roadways ending at her street. There was virtually no traffic in the Berkeley Hills since the homes had emptied out.

Something caught her eye. She angled the bike up a dirt road that led between rows of a ruined apple orchard and doused the lights. She pulled magic to hide the heat signature from her engine and got off the bike, barely allowing herself to breathe. The growl of reciprocating engines grew louder. Heat-seeking radar pinged off the ward she'd erected around herself and her bike. Kate forced herself to stand her ground. The pull of her cat form was strong, but she ignored it. Her best chance was to sneak out of Berkeley as a human. If she took to her animal form, she'd be stuck in the woods and less than useless to Devon.

Her heart seized in her chest when she thought of him, and her eyes ached with unshed tears. What the hell had happened? Had they beaten the truth out of him and dumped him in prison? Had they killed him like they did the other shifters to spare themselves the expense of keeping him locked up?

I can't think that way. I have to believe he's still alive.

She reached for him through the mate bond. Nothing. Kate tried again, but her magic was absorbed by something. Probably not safe to keep broadcasting—if a black hole was out there sucking up her energy and her location.

An idea slammed her between the eyes. If she'd had other shifter partners, she would've thought of it sooner. Kate focused on the roadway a hundred yards from her. The lights from two trucks lit the night, then passed by. It was time to go, but she took a moment to commune with her cat. She was breaking shifter rules about maintaining the integrity of each of her forms, but she was scared and desperate.

"Find Devon's cat. He'll know if Devon is still alive. No matter what the news, tell me."

"But—"

"I know it's against the rules. Just do it. I tried the mate bond and came up dry."

Her cat growled. *"I love him too. If he has been damaged, we will kill who is responsible."*

Kate sent power spinning downhill to see if any other vehicles were approaching. She couldn't hear any, but it paid to be extra careful. There wasn't much time. Once the police discovered her house was empty, they'd come racing after her, and she didn't want to end up trapped between cops above and below.

She straddled the bike without starting its engine and let it coast downhill. It went just as fast as it would have if she'd fired the engine, but without a damning heat signature trail to follow. In a few minutes, she merged with other traffic and felt safe enough to engage the engine.

She wanted to go by her office and destroy her hard drive there, but it was too dangerous. If they wanted her badly enough to storm her house, it was a good bet cops would be waiting at her office. She worked at moving beyond her fear to develop a viable plan. The shifter underground had a headquarters, but she didn't know where it was. Information like that was on a need to know basis.

Kate glanced at her wrist computer. She should chuck it. They could trace her through the electronics. Part of her was surprised they hadn't done that first. Maybe they'd been so confident they'd trap her at home, it hadn't occurred to them. She pulled to the corner, parked her bike, and ducked into a bar. In moments, she'd sold her wrist computer for black market cash. She clicked a few buttons to erase its data, handed it over to its new owner, and fled.

Her next stop was in the seedy section of downtown. She drove up and down streets blazing with neon and finally picked a likely establishment with the help of her cat senses and shifter magic. They ran true. In less than five minutes, she was out the door with a brand new wrist computer.

The proprietor assured her it was untraceable. It cost five hundred credits in black market cash, but she had thousands in her escape suitcase. Kate snorted. The man who ran the shop had looked her over appraisingly, licked his lips, and offered to drop a hundred credits off the price if she'd service him. She'd tried to look flattered, told him she might if she weren't in a rush, and counted bills into his grimy hand. No point in antagonizing him. If she ended up on the run for an extended period of time, she might need him again.

The rush of cool, night air was welcome on her overheated face. Kate tapped Max's number and waited. She kept her visor up so he'd recognize her through the vid feed. It was late, past midnight. She hated to wake him, but…

"Roman," he snapped. "What?"

"I need to hide. Things have gone to hell."

"What are you calling me on?"

"Don't worry. It's not traceable. I just bought it."

Breath whistled loud in her ear. "Shit. I heard something went down at police headquarters, but I didn't want to look too interested. Go to…" He rattled off an address in Hayward. "Tonight's code is—" papers rustled "—nightshade. Knock twice, give them the code, and they'll let you in."

"Can you find out if—?"

"Get some sleep, Roman. I'll talk with you in the morning."

She stared at the display. He'd ended the contact. Kate blew out a breath and looked around her. It was a while since she'd had to navigate on her own without the benefit of her car's onboard computer. She turned hard left and headed for the expressway. Her hands gripped the controls so hard they hurt. She forced herself to relax.

"He lives," sounded deep in her mind. *"We will save him."*

"Yes, we will." Kate was so relieved, she stated shaking.

"Devon's cat is ready to fight. So are the rest of us."

"I'm heading to safety for tonight. Tomorrow, we'll come up with a plan."

"Once you are safe, come to me."

"I will."

Something close to hysteria raced along her nerve endings. Kate wanted to turn the bike around, storm the police department—or the prison—and wrest her love from wherever they'd locked him up, but that was foolhardy. She'd be throwing her life away and not helping him at all.

"Hold on, Devon," she projected, hoping against hope, it would somehow get through. *"I will get you out of there."*

~

THE ADDRESS MAX gave her was in Hayward's sprawling warehouse district. It was badly signed but she didn't want to risk feeding the address into the nav app on her wrist computer. Finally, she found the right place, got off her bike, and unstrapped her bag. She took off her helmet and locked it to the bike. Her legs were wobbly, and a headache pounded behind one eye. She rapped twice on a corrugated metal door.

"Password," sounded in mind speech.

She gave it. The door rumbled open just far enough for her to squeeze through.

"Follow the light." A voice with metallic undertones reverberated all around her.

What light?

She gazed into the gloom, then dialed in her cat vision. A pale green LED blinked at floor level. She walked to it. Another lit a few feet ahead. As she followed the series of lights, she was pleased the underground was so cautious. If she hadn't been a shifter, she wouldn't even have heard the password request. Human vision couldn't see the particular light frequency showing her the way. She wondered if they altered it for different shifter species.

"Stop."

Kate glanced up. She'd been so focused on the floor, she'd nearly walked into a stainless steel door. It whooshed open. She stepped inside. The door shut, and the metal cage she stood in plummeted downward. An elevator. She rubbed her forehead to ease her headache. Something tight coiled deep inside her began to relax. Kate started to believe she might be safe, at least for tonight.

If she was safe, it meant she could pull out all the stops to rescue Devon from whatever hell he'd fallen into.

The door opened onto a well-lit corridor. A tall man carrying an assault rifle barred her way. Red hair spilled down his shoulders. Faded Levis and a flannel shirt clung to an impressively muscled frame. Hard, cold, hazel eyes radiated danger. "Shift," he growled. "It's the last test. Then I will show you to your room—if you pass. If you don't, you're a dead woman."

Kate dropped her bag. "Mind if I get out of these clothes? No point ruining them."

"Do what you have to. I'm immune to seduction attempts, so don't waste your energy."

"I'm mated. Don't waste yours." She tugged off her jacket and let it fall atop her bag. Her shirt followed. She kicked off her boots and slithered out of her jeans and panties. She heard a sharp intake of breath. Maybe rifle-boy wasn't as immune as he liked to think he was.

Kate reached for her cat form and felt the transformation lengthen her torso and draw her legs under her. She padded around the man and snuffled him shamelessly.

He snorted. "Hussy."

She purred. Despite everything, the sheer joy of her cat form filled her. Apparently the man sensed it. He bent to retrieve her things. "Follow me."

Kate loped down the long corridor until it dead ended, then looked over one shoulder at him, whiskers twitching. *"Which way?"*

"Right. Second door."

She moved to the indicated place and stopped. He laid a palm on a pad next to the door. It opened onto a well-appointed bedroom, decorated in Holiday Inn modern. Comfy and functional. He dropped her things on the bed and pulled a robe off a hook in the closet. "I need you back in human form to program the lock. Also I need to show you where the cafeteria is."

"May I have a few minutes with my cat? I promised her."

"Sure. Be back for you in five." He faded out the door and pulled it shut behind him.

By the time he knocked, she was ready, robe belted tightly around her. Her cat side didn't have any further news about Devon other than his cat tried to access him without success. Maybe he was too scared to shift. Or in a place where he couldn't. Or shackled. Cats hated iron. All shifter animal forms did. They'd resist the transformation if it meant the touch of it against their fur.

The man with red hair stuck out a hand. "I'm Ryan."

She took his hand. "Kate."

"Yes, I know. Max called us about you."

She quirked a brow. "Even with that, you put me through my paces."

He shrugged. "Can't be too careful. Someone could have impersonated you through the vid feed to Max. It's possible to manipulate images and voice patterns. Put your hand on the plate."

He clicked buttons on a handheld console. "All set. Follow me. Are you hungry?"

"Not particularly." She trailed after him. "But I probably should eat something."

"Cafeteria's here. Computer room is just across the hall." He placed his palm on the same type of glass plate that sat next to her door. "Now that you've been programmed into the system, you'll have access to all the common areas. We're set up for long term residency—"

"No." She clutched his arm. "I have to free Devon."

Ryan shook his head sharply. "We will move on our enemy using a coordinated approach. To do anything different jeopardizes us all." He pried her fingers off his arm and propelled her into the dining room. A bank of glass-fronted food dispensers lined one wall.

Kate gazed around the room. Half a dozen shifters hunched over plates and cups in a room large enough to accommodate fifty. Metal tables for four were scattered throughout the space. Large screens lined the upper part of the walls. A soccer game played on one, an older movie on another. She sank into a chair.

Ryan clucked over her like a mother hen, went to the glass wall, and returned with two cups of coffee. He dropped packets of powdered creamer and sugar in front of her along with a plastic spoon. "Want something to go with it?" His voice was gruff.

"Uh, soup maybe. And some bread."

"What kind?"

"Surprise me." She took a sip of coffee. Hot and fresh, it wasn't bad. He placed a bowl in front of her and returned a few minutes later with a roll and butter. Kate sniffed the soup. It looked like some variant of chicken with vegetables and noodles floating in it. She spooned some into her mouth. Like the coffee, it tasted freshly made. Her stomach clenched, and she realized she was hungry.

He unslung his rifle from his shoulder, laid it on one of the empty chairs, and sat across from her. "Good you're eating. You'll need fuel."

"Why? What's happening?"

"Max is worried. Seems the police department in Berkeley herded the entire Tracker task force into some sort of lockdown. They sounded the alarm, so other law enforcement agencies are following suit. Those men are too valuable to lose. We need them on our side." He twisted a corner of his mouth into a wry frown. "In many ways, this isn't a bad turn of events. After being imprisoned, the cops won't feel kindly disposed toward their bosses, and once we spring them—"

"—they won't be nearly as conflicted about throwing their lot in with us." She ginned up a wan smile. "Food helps. Thanks."

"Don't mention it. I've got to get moving. Back on patrol. Oh yes, your bike. Moved it inside after I left you in your room. Rear wheel was locked. Had to lift it. Oomph."

"Thanks. I was worried someone would steal it."

His chair made a squeaking sound when he pushed it back. "Get some sleep. Max will be here sometime tomorrow morning to talk with everyone. We'll let you know when."

"How many of us are here?"

"A few hundred."

Her eyes widened. "No shit."

Ryan laughed. "No shit. You'll meet everyone, or most of us anyway, tomorrow." He turned and walked from the room.

Kate finished her food. She got a refill on her coffee, found a gooey brownie in the food case, and took both back to her quarters. She juggled the brownie plate into the curve of one arm to free her right hand for the keypad. A gentle shove from her foot once she was inside, and the door snicked shut.

She set her food on a small desk and sank onto the bed. Devon. It felt wrong for her to be safe and comfortable when he was locked up. Pain shot through her, the sensation so intense she curled into a ball. She thought about his arms around her and his lips on hers. Beautiful dark brown eyes brimming with love danced in her memory.

She grabbed a pillow and hugged it close to have something to hold. If the unspeakable happened and the bastards killed him, she'd stop at nothing to gain revenge.

"I'll blow up the fucking world, if that's what it takes," she muttered through clenched teeth. Deep in her mind, her cat growled agreement.

CHAPTER 12

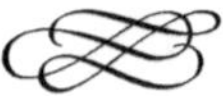

*D*evon leaned against the brick wall of the holding pen under the police station. He'd told Captain Aaron pretty much everything. The only things he'd glossed over were the fact that he'd shifted and the depth of his feelings for Kate. He'd avoided mentioning the shifter underground at all. The rest of the Tracker task force was locked in the underground room with him. Voices rose and fell; most of them buzzed with anger. Devon was good at fading out of sight. It was an old Native American trick that urged people to look elsewhere.

He was worried sick about Kate. His boss knew she was a shifter. When Devon denied it after tracking her that day, all he'd done was cast suspicion on himself. Apparently the police had known about her for quite a while. They'd left her alone until she started harboring shifter fugitives. Devon didn't ask, but the implication was more than one officer had availed himself of her services. He'd tried to warn her just before Captain Aaron ripped his wrist computer off his arm and pressed the two buttons that would wipe its drive. The odds of her looking at her screen at just that moment were slim.

His hands ached. He unclenched his fists and gazed at the crowd.

He had to escape. Kate needed him. Maybe if he got the other officers riled up enough, they could bludgeon their way out. Especially if they summoned their animal forms. He strode to the front of the room.

"There you are," one man yelled. The crowd surged forward.

"Yeah, he's why we got stuck in here," someone else cried.

Devon held up both hands. "Give me five minutes. If you still want to pound me to a bloody pulp, I won't fight you. But first." He heaved a chair at a blinking red LED that was probably a microphone. It shattered. "See any more of them?"

Breaking glass sounded from the back of the room. "Got it," a voice with a strong Middle Eastern accent called out.

"Your five minutes just started, Heartshorn." Someone elbowed him in the ribs, and then jumped out of reach.

Devon detailed the effects of the serum on those with shifter blood. He recited the forty-two names from memory. Tanaka would have been the forty-third.

"My name ain't on that list. How come I'm here?" a gaunt blond cop demanded.

Devon nodded. "That's correct. Seven of us don't have a drop of shifter blood. I have no idea why they chucked you in here with the rest of us."

"How come you know all this stuff?" the blond officer asked.

"Because I shifted just like Tanaka, and it scared the crap out of me. I started running down leads to find out more when the captain called me in. How about the rest of you? Anyone feel like confessing? I only had twenty-five-percent shifter blood, but all it takes is ten to shove you over the edge once you've had that series of infusions."

The crowd milled about, rearranging itself. The seven non-shifters gathered in a corner, their heads bent together.

"Has anybody had any unusual experiences since they got the infusions?" Devon pressed, raising his hand to set an example. Around the room, hands edged up. Once the men saw they weren't the only ones, more hands joined in. "I'd say that's about three-quarters of us. Have all of you shifted, or is it just hypersensitive smell and hearing, and animal dreams?"

One of the non-shifters strode to Devon's side. Medium height, with long brown hair and blue eyes, he stuck out a hand. "Robert Tabor."

Devon shook it. "Nice to meet you." He waited, unsure what the other man wanted.

"Before you go any further with this, we—" he gestured to the small group in the back of the room "—decided to help you. We're mad as hell we got shanghaied. We also don't think any of you should be punished. After all, it was their fucking drug that did this. We all had to agree to it in order to be on the task force. I'd say this is a brass problem. And a scientist problem. They caused it. They can fix it. What are they going to do with all of you? Take you out and shoot you? Dump you in prison? I call bullshit."

A roar rose from the men. Fists pumped the air. Devon smiled grimly and waved his hands for silence.

"I think we can get out of here. I asked before, how many of you have shifted?"

The tally was thirty, fairly evenly split between bears, wolves, coyotes, and mountain cats. Devon squared his shoulders and wished desperately that he knew more. "This will be the blind leading the blind," he began, "but I need you to practice shifting so you get more comfortable with how to go from your human form to your animal one. Shuck your clothes. No point in wrecking them. Let down your guard. Your animal will find you…"

An hour later, energy fairly buzzed through the room. "Damned shame about Tanaka," another Asian cop murmured. "If he could've held on, he'd still be alive."

"Yeah, his wife too," someone chimed in.

Guilt pierced Devon. He should've tried harder. Kate had wanted to, but he couldn't get out of there fast enough once he heard Tanaka's wife suggest seppuku. Not that they'd done the whole sword disembowelment thing, but still…

He faced the crowd. "If we can get out of here, we need a plan now that you've developed some ability to move from human to animal and back again."

"You mentioned some sort of shifter underground," someone said. "Maybe we could go there."

"Yeah, if I knew where it was." He thought about his conversation with Max. Maybe all wasn't lost. "They may find us, but we'll need a place to regroup. Ideas?"

A beefy, middle-aged man with a bald head and warm brown eyes nodded. "Uh, got a cousin who's part of the mob. They hate the law. They'd take us in, at least for a while." He sketched out directions to a tenement in Oakland. "Looks like shit from the outside, but that's just a front to discourage visitors."

"They might let you in," someone yelled, "but what about the rest of us?"

"Heh," the bald man muttered. "Good point. I'd call, but they took my electronics. Guess you'll have to wait for me at the corner. There's an abandoned building just north of there."

"No offense, Bolton, but what if you don't make it? It ain't like the brass are just gonna lean back and let the lot of us waltz out of here."

No, they aren't.

Devon wondered how many of these men—he was starting to look at them as his men—would die. "If Bolton doesn't show, you'll meet there anyway. You'll need clothes and shoes and black market cash. Anything you can pick up along the way will help. If you've worked undercover, you'll have connections. Don't be shy about using them. Don't wait for me. The captain put out the call to pick up my woman. I have to help her if I can."

He inhaled sharply. "Listen up. Whoever said that about Bolton maybe not getting out alive made a good point. It's dangerous to leave. No one has to. It's up to you. If you want to make a break for it, the more of us there are, the better the odds, but no one will hold it against you if you opt out. That's especially true for the ones without any shifter blood."

"We're all in," Tabor growled. "We talked about it."

"Yeah, and furthermore—" the gaunt, blond cop stepped forward "—even if they let us out of this shithole, we're all going to quit anyway. Bastards. How can we work for arbitrary assholes like that?"

What an incredible group of men. Devon wished he had time to get to know them better.

Maybe I still can.

He examined the lock holding the metal door in place. "Does anyone know much about this holding tank?"

"Why?" The nearest officer walked over, naked and barefoot, and bent to look closely at the lock. "Son of a bitch. I don't think it's electronic."

"My take exactly. How about if one of you bears takes a crack at it." He repeated himself in mind speech.

A grizzly lumbered forward and drew his front leg back.

"Wait." Devon turned to the others. "Find your animal forms. You have a better chance in them because you can run faster, and you'll scare the shit out of whoever's after you. You can shift back once you're clear of the station."

"We'll be naked."

"True enough." Devon grinned. "This is Berkeley, home of the weird. No one will probably even notice."

He nodded to the grizzly and claimed his cat form. A single paw stroke broke the lock. Men and animals surged forward.

"Halt or I'll shoot." Two officers jumped in front of them.

Weapon fire reverberated in the hallway. The *phut* of lasers and the *ping* of live ammo made Devon's skin crawl. His cat form liked bullets even less than he did. Shrieks, snarls, and hisses tore into Devon's soul. He jumped a guard and batted him hard enough to knock him out. He wasn't ready to kill—not yet. If Kate was injured or dead, though, all bets were off.

Something hot seared his side. He couldn't stop to check his injury. A laser had grazed him, hopefully nothing worse. Devon raced through the door leading to the underground parking garage. Tabor had his hand on the electronic plate to keep it open. His chest bloomed red just as Devon leapt through the door.

It was foolhardy, but he wanted to go back. To shift and scoop Tabor up and see he got to a hospital, but his cat urged him on. He hit street level and ran fast enough to match the traffic. His side burned. He ignored it. Once he'd put a few blocks between him and the station, he ducked into an alley. A couple of winos screamed and bolted for the street.

Bet they'll think it's the worst case of DTs they ever had.

He reached for his human form. Broken glass cut into his feet. He looked at his side. A long red welt oozed blood. More than oozed. It dripped in a steady stream. He culled through a trash bin, found a filthy robe, and tied it around him. It stank of vomit. He walked gingerly out of the alley. Once he hit the city streets, he shambled into a jog. His house was only a mile or so away. The odds of the cops staking it out were thin, what with so many of them on the run. He needed clothing and money and first aid supplies to clean his wound. Once he had those, he'd buy another wrist computer and work on finding Kate.

Sirens blared. Devon ducked into another alley. *Crap.* Maybe this would be harder than he thought. He said a silent prayer, hoping most of them had made it and struck out again for home. It was nearly dark. He stuck to the shadows and used his Native American skills to blend into the darkness.

By the time he turned down his street, his feet were killing him and his side burned. The ratty robe was soaked with blood. He felt lightheaded. He crawled over his back fence and dug the spare key out of a flowerpot. Devon let himself inside and fell face down on his kitchen floor. Consciousness flirted with him, before it slipped away.

~

HE DIDN'T KNOW how long he was passed out, only that he lay in a pool of congealed blood. His blood. Moonlight filtered through the kitchen windows. "Goddamn it." His voice sounded rusty to him. "After all that, I am not going to die here."

He grasped the edge of the counter and hauled himself upright. Untying the robe, he dropped it on the floor. Naked, he turned the water on and washed his wound. It seemed clean enough except for whatever vermin had been in the robe. About eight inches long, blood seeped the minute he took pressure off it. In the old days before lasers, razor wounds used to look like that.

Devon grabbed a bottle of whiskey from the ledge, uncapped it with his teeth, and poured it down his side to sterilize things, gasping in pain. He spit out the cap and took a couple of swallows from the bottle, welcoming the burn as the liquor hit his stomach. That done, he clumped heavily to the bathroom and piled gauze squares over his open flesh. He wound a large elasticized bandage around his torso, securing it with metal butterfly strips.

He rustled through his medicine cabinet and found a nearly full bottle of antibiotics from when he'd had an abscessed tooth. Popping two into his mouth, he swallowed them dry. He set the bottle on the ledge, planning to take it with him. Maybe it wasn't the right antibiotic, but at least it was better than nothing—he hoped.

Because he was on the move, his head felt clearer. He rinsed the stink of the robe off himself with a washcloth and got dressed, amazed Captain Aaron hadn't shown up on his doorstep. Devon debated taking his personal car. He'd be safer on foot, but he didn't feel all that steady. He scooped up his pills, his black market cash, and some food, took a healthy swig from the whiskey bottle and clattered down his back steps. He backtracked for water. He had to be dehydrated from losing blood. He drank a quart standing at the sink, filled two poly bottles, and took them with him.

He told the car's nav system to take him to the electronics shop he'd visited after he'd seen Dr. Adams. It was four in the morning, but their sign had advertised they never closed.

The proprietor, a different clerk than last time, whistled when Devon pushed the swinging door inward and strode inside. "Looks like you ran up against a gorilla and lost, dude." The clerk's long black hair was pulled into a ponytail, making his high cheekbones and beak of a nose stand out. He looked Native American just like Devon.

"Not funny."

"Wasn't trying to be. What can I help you with?"

"I want that one." Devon pointed to a wrist computer in a locked glass case. The clerk got it out and launched into a sales pitch. Devon cut him off. "How much?"

"Four hundred credits. Black market only."

Devon checked to see the computer was complete with case, charger, and plug-ins. He counted out bills and walked out of the store. Apparently price was a fluctuating commodity in places like that.

Next time, I'll barter with the guy.

He drove a few blocks to one of the public library branches and parked. Libraries always had parking, especially in the middle of the night. No one read anymore.

He tapped Kate's number into the display. A tinny recording, *This number is offline,* jolted him. He tried her home and got the same recording. Her office still had her voice cheerfully telling him to leave a message. He hit the disconnect key. If her home and wrist computers were defunct, no way she'd be checking her office voice mail, but the cops might.

He sucked air, trying to think. If he had Max's number, he would've called him. He castigated himself for not getting it from Kate. He thought about calling the Governor's office, but knew how stupid that would be. No one would be there at this hour. Even if they were, Max wouldn't talk with him—not from his day job.

Because he had to do something—stewing in his own angst was killing him—he programmed Kate's address into the car's computer. Maybe there'd be some clues at her house. If they'd apprehended her there—or worse—he was pretty certain he'd find a trail.

He forced himself to drink water and eat processed cheese, crackers, and cookies while his car picked the best route to get across town. He took the car off autopilot as it climbed higher into the Berkeley Hills. When he was still three or four blocks away, he hunted for a place to stash his car far enough off the roadway it couldn't be seen. A dirt road wound off to his right. He pulled as far as he could into what had once been an apple orchard and killed his motor.

Devon tucked his hair under a cap. He bent to smear dirt on his face. Nothing he could do about his height and broad shoulders. They were a dead giveaway if he ran into any cops who knew him. He started toward the road when his cat kicked up a fuss. It wanted out. Now. Devon thought about the logistics of removing his bandage and suggested a compromise. The cat's senses flooded him.

He hadn't spent enough time in his cat form to be truly conversant with either it or the ways he could tap into its abilities while still human. He made a commitment to remedy that as soon as he found Kate and things settled a bit.

Devon inhaled sharply. Kate. No wonder his cat had pitched a fit. Kate had been here. Well, maybe not here exactly, but close by. And not so long ago. He walked carefully down the dirt road, feline vision glued to the ground, nostrils flaring. He found motorcycle tracks and footprints. He knelt and sniffed. Yes, they were her footprints. She'd stood here.

He straightened. Joy swooped through him. He wanted to screech *thank you* to whichever god had let her see his warning, but silence served his purposes better. They hadn't caught her. She'd gotten at least this far, which meant she'd probably given the bastards the slip.

He glanced toward her house. Was it still worth visiting? As long as he was this close, he might as well. Maybe he could find Max's contact information.

Devon circled uphill carefully, keeping to the woods behind the deserted houses across the street from Kate's. No point walking into a trap. He kept the cat's senses front and center, using them to ferret out danger. He wished he understood the shifter magic Kate told him about, but right now anything more difficult than sneaking uphill was beyond him. He still felt weak and disoriented from his wound. Sleep would help.

No. No sleep until I find Kate.

His brief stint passed out on the kitchen floor would have to be enough.

He stayed hidden in trees across from her house for long minutes. Nothing moved. He sucked in a steadying breath, scenting the air. Smells bombarded him, none of them human. Devon crept forward. He headed for Kate's back door, using clumps of trees and large rocks for cover. Another thirty feet and he'd have it. Then he could pick the lock and—

"I knew you'd show up here. Freeze or I'll blast you to hell after the mess you made of my station house," Captain Aaron's unmistakable voice yelled.

Devon straightened from his crouch, hands over his head.

His cat screamed imprecations. It wanted to kill the bastard. *"Kill him now, goddamn it."*

Devon gauged the distance between him and Captain Aaron, mind racing as he tried to map out a defense. He cursed himself for not bringing a weapon. That oversight might be his undoing. And Kate's.

After today's escape, they'd chuck him in solitary and throw away the key. Or maybe just kill him outright. He eyed a pile of decorative boulders. He could dive behind them and chuck smaller rocks at his boss.

"How'd you mask your scent, Captain?" Devon made the question casual and edged closer to the rocks that might save his life.

"That information's classified. You're not on the force anymore." Lance Aaron stepped from the shadows behind Kate's house, assault rifle leveled at Devon's chest. "It's a damned shame, son. You were a good cop. I liked you, but I won't tolerate insubordination."

"I wasn't insubordinate. I took your fucking drug. If you wouldn't have forced me, we wouldn't be here."

"No comment."

A faint rustle pricked Devon's enhanced senses. *Crap.* Did Captain Aaron have reinforcements stashed somewhere? Made sense. He probably wasn't working alone. Devon's heart sped up; his throat tightened. Maybe his boulder strategy wouldn't work after all. Not if he had to ward off multiple assailants.

From out of nowhere, a bear, a mountain lion, and a coyote converged on the captain, bellies low to the earth. He spun, rifle firing wildly, but his aim was high, and he was a shade too late. The animals leapt on him from three sides and drove him to the ground. The weapon skittered out of his hands. Devon dove on top of it and rolled. His side screeched in protest. He jumped to his feet, rifle in hand, and aimed it at Aaron's head.

"Call off your shifter buddies," Captain Aaron shouted. "That's an order, Heartshorn."

"Really?" Devon strode closer and stood over his former boss. "You just told me I was off the force. That means I don't have to follow your orders anymore. Too bad, Aaron."

"I'll reinstate you. We'll forget any of this happened. I'll, ah, even take Roman off the shifter list."

"Don't grovel. There was a time I respected you." Devon glanced at the three shifters and made a chopping motion with one hand. "Go for it, buddies."

Devon let himself into Kate's house. A long drawn-out scream followed him. It ended in a gurgling retch. Probably someone had driven a claw through the captain's larynx to shut him up.

Devon's eyes widened when he saw the wreckage of Kate's living room. Christ! Her house had been ransacked. He heard claws on the back stairs and turned. "Thank you, whoever you are. You saved my life."

The bear ambled close. *"We're friends of Kate's. That's all you need to know."*

"Yes." The coyote padded up. *"We were nearby, on our way to visit her, when she took off out of here like a bat fleeing hell. Soon after, the cops came and tore things up. I wanted to kill them, but these two held me back."*

Hope surged. Devon asked, "Do you know where Kate is?"

The mountain cat joined the other two. *"No. We were hoping you did."*

Devon's cat purred. It wanted out to play.

The others must've sensed it. *"Shift and run with us,"* the bear invited.

"I can't. I'm hurt. If I take the bandage off, I'll bleed more. And I have to find Kate." An idea formed. "Do any of you know how I can contact Max?"

"Yes." The coyote yipped several times. *"If you get a chance to shift, do it. Your cat heals faster than your human form. In terms of Max..."*

DEVON WHISTLED as he trotted back to his car, rifle slung over a shoulder. Ammo rattled in his pockets. He'd taken everything useful he could from the captain. The three shifters had regained their human forms and dragged Lance Aaron's body away. They'd assured him it would disappear without a trace. The bear had been a chemical engineer before he was imprisoned. He'd do something to obliterate the captain's blood. Devon had told him to either do it fast or not at all. It wouldn't be long before squad cars showed up.

Dawn lightened the sky in the east. He got behind the wheel and tapped Max's number into his wrist computer, then eased his car down the rutted lane. Best to put some distance between himself and the Berkeley Hills and lose himself in the city's traffic. Captain Aaron would have left his plans with the desk commander. When his life force indicator blinked out on the motherboard, reinforcements would converge on Kate's house.

Place your thumb on the screen and wait, flared across the display. Max's brusque voice followed. "Devon. I see where you are. Did you have anything to do with the cop who was just murdered up there?"

"Do you have time for me to start at the beginning?"

"If you can do it in less than five minutes. I need a chance to tell you where to go and fill you in on what will happen next. That's more important right now than why Lance Aaron is dead."

"Yes, sir. Just cut me off when you've heard enough." Devon cleared his throat and started talking.

CHAPTER 13

Kate didn't think she'd be able to sleep. She'd taken her cat form, paced worriedly, then reverted to human and huddled on her bed, eyes dry and burning. The cycle repeated endlessly, so it surprised her when her wrist computer buzzed, dragging her from an exhausted sleep.

She grappled for it and peered at the display. Just past six. "Max?" She forced her fuzzy brain into motion.

"I'm not slated to get much sleep tonight. Misery loves company."

Her fingers spasmed around the computer. "Devon. I know he's alive, but have you heard anything?"

"You forget yourself, Roman. I ask the questions." His voice softened. "Yeah, he's fine. Wouldn't be if he hadn't run into your last three housemates, though. They saved his bacon."

She wanted to ask if Max could bring Devon in, but bit back the words. He'd called her for a reason. If she waited, he'd tell her what it was.

"Did you look at the list of names on that task force when Heartshorn gave it to you?" His voice was brusque.

"Yes. I didn't study it or anything, but—"

"Don't take this wrong, Roman, but how many of those men were your clients?"

She resurrected the list in her mind. "Maybe ten or twelve. Possibly a few more. I didn't look at it for all that long, but some of the names were familiar. For the more common ones, it might not be the same guy, though."

"They're holed up in Oakland. The ones who weren't killed in yesterday's shootout, that is. Heartshorn's headed their way now. We need to get them to safety. But first someone has to assess which ones won't turn double and fuck us. Since you already had a relationship with some of them where they trusted you with their, ahem—" he cleared his throat "—secrets, you're a logical choice. Plus, I figure you'll nag me to death until you're reunited with Devon. I know how relentless mated pairs can be."

She waved a hand over the bedside lamp. It illuminated, casting shadows on bland cream-colored walls. "Tell me where."

"Oakland warehouse district. Go to the seediest part and…"

Her heart sang. Happiness thrummed from her belly to the tips of her fingers and toes. Devon. She'd be with him again soon. Deep inside, her cat yowled its joy and urged her to hurry.

"…be careful until you clear Berkeley. City'll be crawling with cops. They don't like to lose one of their own, especially their commanding officers. You're on their hit list, Roman. Don't forget it."

"On my way."

A sharp rap sounded on her door.

Max must've heard it too. "That would be Ryan. I called him just before you. He'll see you have a clean vehicle to drive. Also, he'll be your contact through this operation. Be sure to get his computer codes." The screen grayed out.

She dropped her wrist computer on the bed and sprinted for the door. It opened before she got to it.

"You decent?" Ryan grinned at her, taking in her thin robe. "Think I liked the view better when you were naked."

She stuck out her tongue. "Give me a couple seconds, I'll get dressed."

He handed her a stack of folded clothes. "Put these on. They'll blend in better than what you were wearing last night. Not so form-fitting. You do not want to draw attention."

"Are you going to stand there and watch?"

He turned around. "Better?"

She shinnied into underwear, dark sweats, and a dark watch cap. Socks and boots followed. "Okay. Ready."

"Not quite." He walked toward her. "Sit in one of those chairs. I need to work on your face."

He wrapped her hair close around her head, pinned it, and put the cap back in place. Next, he attacked her face with makeup, brushes, and sponges. "Once you get back here, we need to dye your hair. It stands out like a sore thumb." He fussed for a bit, and then stood back. "Step into the bathroom, and tell me what you think."

Kate gasped. Her mouth hung open. She shut it with a clack. The face staring at her in the mirror looked older, haggard. Lines spiraled out from her nose and mouth. He'd managed to nearly obliterate the sharp angles of her cheekbones and jaw. Between that and her own illusory magic, even a close friend might not recognize her.

"Christ, you must have been a makeup artist."

"Good guess, Sherlock. I worked in Hollywood before we had to go into hiding." He placed the makeup kit on a table and crooked a finger. "Up and at 'em. Max likes it when we're punctual." Ryan shut the door behind them, bent, and picked up a paper sack. He thrust it at her.

"What's that?"

"Breakfast. I put a cup of coffee in the car."

She laughed. "Wow! You're better than a butler."

He laughed right along with her. "I aim to please, ma'am."

Her boot heels clicked on the hard floor. Next time she came down this hall, Devon would be by her side. She'd drag him into her room and—"

"This way. Garage is underground just like everything else."

With her destination programmed into the onboard computer, and transcribed into her wrist computer just in case, Kate let the car decide how to get to Oakland. Nav systems had gotten better. They employed a complicated metric that looked at traffic, road construction, type of vehicle, percent grade on hills, and a few other things before picking a route.

The dashboard display lit with *Police Vehicle Approaching*. Kate disengaged the nav system and pulled to the curb. She averted her head and strengthened the illusion she was an older woman. A police vehicle screamed past, followed by another.

Sweat beaded her brow. Were they hunting for her? Or was it some other poor, hapless shifter who'd drawn their attention? She made a rude sound, merged into the flow of cars, and reset the autopilot. Maybe they were after a real criminal for a change. What a refreshing change of pace that would be.

Even with the hundred-mile-an-hour speed limit on the expressway, it still took her over an hour to get to Oakland. Cars were backed up for long stretches where no one moved. All vehicles except law and emergency had to be electric to preserve what was left of the air quality. Some of their batteries died while they waited, clogging the lanes even further.

Kate chafed. She could've gotten to her destination faster on foot. Not really, but almost. She'd asked Max for Devon's contact code, but he'd turned her down. "He'll be busy," Max had snapped. "You'll see him soon enough."

"The way things are going, maybe not," she muttered through clenched teeth.

When the car rolled into a rundown neighborhood filled with boarded-up tenements, she checked the address against the one in her computer. She was in the right place, but it didn't feel safe to get out of her car. She glanced about. Where could she even leave the car? From the looks of things, it would be either vandalized or stolen the minute she walked away from it.

At least parking was plentiful. She shot Ryan a quick text.

His answer was, *Do what you have to. Don't worry about the car. We can send another or a hovercraft to pick you up.*

Movement caught her eye. A young thug chased another, hit him in the head with a brick, grabbed his wallet, and ran. Kate scrambled out of her car, locked it, and raced to the victim. He was unconscious. Blood poured down his face. Her heart ached. He didn't look much more than twelve. She dialed the emergency access code on his wrist computer. It would transmit his location.

Kate thought about staying with him, but didn't feel all that secure out in the open. If the cops had put out an ABP on her, she wasn't safe anywhere.

She patted his hand, told him help was on the way even though she knew he couldn't hear her, and jogged to the address she'd been given. She had to be careful mounting the steps since they were rotting away, with gaping holes in the uneven risers. She knocked.

The door opened a few inches. A dark, swarthy man eyed her. "What?"

"I was given this address. Friends of mine are here."

"One of them, eh?" He eyed her. "If you lied and you ain't, I'll have some fun with you."

"Like hell you will."

Desperate to find Devon, Kate pushed past him. Her eyes widened. Once she got away from the entry hall, the interior was in good repair. Smells of mold, mildew, and rotting garbage faded.

She cupped her hands around her mouth. "Devon."

A door slammed. "Aw, Christ! Kate."

Feet pounded toward her. She sprinted in the direction of the sound. Their bodies hurtled together. His arms wrapped around her. She twined hers around him. Breath caught in her throat. Relief so sweet and dizzying she almost passed out sluiced through her.

"Our mated one. It's our mated one," her cat purred.

"You're safe. Thank God you're safe," she said over and over, face buried against his chest. "I've been so scared—"

"I could say the same thing," he murmured against her hair. "Watch my right side."

"Oh my God. Are you hurt?" She stepped back and took a good hard look at him. "Holy crap, you look like hell. Your face is gray, and the skin under your eyes is nearly black. When did you last sleep?"

He gave her a sheepish grin. "Not for the last two nights, that's for sure." His gaze lingered on her. He bent and brushed her lips with his. "I love you, Kate. I was terrified I'd lost you. Did you get my message?"

She nodded, her gaze glued on his. "Luck was with me. It was on my screen for all of a couple of seconds." She touched his cheek. "I love you too. My heart, my life. When you didn't show last night—"

"How do you suppose I felt when my captain sent the dogs after you?" He shook his head. "Hell, I'm so tired, I can barely think. Let's get this over with. Max told me you were coming—and a bunch of other stuff too. I've been worried sick something happened to you. Why'd it take you so long to get here, and who made you up like a circus clown?"

"Traffic was hideous, even worse than usual. The answer to your other question is one of the underground security squad moonlights as a makeup artist." She trotted to keep up with his long-legged stride. "How many of the Tracker squad were killed yesterday?"

"Nine. Six shifters and three humans, if you count Tanaka." He glanced at her, his dark eyes brimming with pain. "Those guys were so courageous. They thought what happened to us was wrong, so they put their lives on the line. That's what cops do when something doesn't resonate."

"So forty-one are left, thirty-seven shifters and four humans."

He nodded. "We did a head count. The missing ones were verified as dead."

Sadness tinged with anger made a spot behind her breastbone ache. Her cat howled mournfully in her mind. Kate clenched her jaw and tried to refocus. "What is this place?"

Devon snorted. "It's a hideout for organized crime. One of the guy's cousins... It doesn't matter. We needed a meeting place. This was better than most because the mob has MD connections. Most of us needed patching up. Everyone's in here." He pushed a door open.

Kate stared. Men sat at tables, or lay on them. Bandages were piled in a corner. A couple of men in blood-spattered blue smocks worked on the injured. Tall, blond, with Nordic features, they could've been twins. The sharp scents of antiseptic and blood blended in an unpleasant mélange. She muted her cat senses. "Have you spoken with the men?"

"I thought I'd wait until the docs were done."

One of the MDs walked to Devon. "Some of these men will need follow-up. We left written orders with each of them."

The other doc came trotting up. He patted Devon's side. "How're those stitches feeling?"

"Uncomfortable, just like you predicted."

"Well, you needed them. Don't forget the antibiotics. You can take the bandage off in two days. No showers until then. Use compresses as hot as you can stand a few times a day after that. Be alert for red streaks or fever. If everything looks good, have someone take the stitches out in seven to ten days."

"Got it. You done here?"

The doctors exchanged glances. "Yeah," the one who'd asked about Devon's stitches said. "Who's going to pay us?"

"How much?" Devon asked.

The men stepped to one side, heads bent together, voices low. One left the room, the other returned to Devon and Kate. "Ten thousand credits. We gave you a break. That barely covers our supplies."

"If you give me an account number—"

The doctor shook his head. "Black market cash only. Last thing we need is an account infusion from a questionable source."

"Will you take a one to one exchange? Dollars for credits?" Kate asked.

"Sure," the doctor replied. "It's close enough."

Kate stepped closer. "I'm sure we can manage that." She sent Ryan a text, looked up from the screen, and met the doctor's blue gaze. "Can you sit tight for half an hour?"

He nodded. She tapped a few more keys. "Okay. A courier will be here soon. He'll come inside."

"Thanks. You have no idea how hard it is to make a living since the government socialized medicine." The MD shot her a blinding smile, then left.

Kate gathered her thoughts. She walked to the front of the room with Devon and waited for him to lead out. He clapped his hands together. The men who'd been talking quieted. "We have safe haven for all of you—"

"What about our wives and kids?" one of the men asked.

"Them too. There's a large safe house that could accommodate all of you and your immediate families. But it will mean you have to drop out of sight. Your kids won't have access to their friends, or their school. You'll effectively disappear. In time, you'll be relocated to other communities elsewhere in the country with new identities."

"You have several options," Kate broke in. "Three, to be precise. You can return to your life. The thirty-seven of you who are shifters can try to manage on your own, but I will tell you that once you've shifted, it's not something you can walk away from."

"Door number two," Devon took over, "is you can go to the safe house without your loved ones. They will eventually believe you've died and move on with their lives. I know that's harsh, but it's the cleanest choice."

"The third option," Kate said, "is we will round up your families and transport them to safe haven where you will be reunited with them."

"Can I talk with my wife first?" a man shouted.

"Unfortunately, no," Devon replied. "I understand that would make it easier, but we can't let people outside our network even know about the existence of shifter safe houses. I'm trusting those of you who choose to return to your lives will keep your mouths shut."

"We won't have a job," someone pointed out.

"Probably not," Devon agreed. "Not after the way we left the station house."

"If we're declared missing or dead," another cop said, his tone reflective, "widows' and orphans' benefits kick in for our wives and kids."

"That's a consideration," someone else muttered.

"Does anyone have questions?" Devon scanned the crowd.

"It's kind of like the witness protection program, but with more rules," a man said.

A corner of Devon's mouth turned down. "You got it."

"Take your time." Kate took a step forward. "But not more than an hour. This isn't the kind of thing that will get easier the longer you think about it. Make your decisions. Devon and I will be over in that corner." She pointed to a table. "Come one by one and let us know. Be forewarned, though. For those of you who pick the safe house, I'll be asking you a bunch of in-depth questions. So will Devon. We can't afford to be compromised."

KATE SLUGGED BACK COLD COFFEE. She met Devon's tired gaze. "That's the last of them. Gee, who would've thought so many would want to sign on? All but three. I tested their answers with magic, and they pinged true."

"I'm surprised too. Crap." He dragged a hand down his face, distorting his features. "What a wretched choice to have to make. The ones leaving their families behind broke my heart." He glanced at the sheet of paper in front of him and counted, "Five men with nine children between them."

"It's more than sad. It's appalling they had to make such a sacrifice. I'm sure some of them took our offer to spare their families the humiliation of being associated with a shifter."

Anger prickled down her spine. She wanted to kill the supercilious bastards who thought they were better just because they were human. "When did we become such pariahs?" Deep inside, her cat yowled its displeasure. Kate shoved her emotions to a back burner so she wouldn't shift, go racing outside, and kill whoever crossed her path. "Guess I ought to text Ryan."

"Yeah, ask him about the humans. I'd love to have them on our side, but make sure it's okay for them to throw their lot in with us. None of them had families. Probably makes the choice easier." He blew out a tense breath. "Speaking of families, I hope the shifters' families don't give us any trouble."

Kate nodded, fingers flying over her display. She looked up. "Max had the same concerns. The families will have an intermediary stopping-off point to double-check there's not an insurrection among any of the wives or kids."

She tapped a few more keys. "Humans are fine." She met Devon's worried gaze. "Ryan will be sending cars at intervals. He estimates it will take twenty-four hours to transport everyone. Do we have enough food?"

Devon nodded. "We'll stay until everyone's left. We need to see this through."

"I'll let the men know. Stretch out on a table." She brushed her fingers over the back of his hand. "Grab some sleep. I'll wake you if I need you." Kate watched him walk to one of the long tables. Love swelled inside her. She longed to lie next to him and hold him close, but that would have to wait.

She glanced at the names on the list in front of her and worried about the three shifters who'd said they couldn't bear to leave their current lives. Kate was certain the police would hunt them down and kill them. They'd be easy enough to find.

She had time—it would be at least an hour before the first transport showed up—so she gathered them and talked about the impossibility of maintaining their current day-to-day lives. They faced almost certain imprisonment or death. She also touched on genetics and the odds their children might either be shifters or could turn into shifters with a little assistance from the infusion.

"Why would they want to?" a young, redheaded officer asked. "It's like signing up for a life in Hell."

Kate's eyes flashed. "No, it's not. We have magic. Our animals are strong and beautiful and wise. If humans knew what they were missing, they'd kill to be like us." She took a breath. "What's disappeared since the government turned us into persona non grata is our pride in what we are. We used to have that in spades before some cretin decided we were dangerous. Shit. When I got out of the car today, a human kid ran another one down and bashed his skull in. For every shifter who got out of control and harmed a human, there have been a thousand humans who did the same thing."

"She's right," the officer muttered. "Okay," he met her gaze, hazel eyes troubled. "I'm in." A corner of his mouth turned down. "Hope my wife doesn't kill me."

"Those of you with families will have a transitional stopping-off point to sort things out—"

"Why didn't you say that before?" an older Asian man asked.

"Because I didn't know."

"In that case, I'm in."

"Me, too," the third cop, an East Indian, chimed with a mild British accent.

Thank God.

Kate let her eyes close for a moment. "Great, I'll let the underground know. Each of you is valuable. We need your talents. We have work for you."

"Thank you," the Asian murmured. "My biggest worry was how I was going to make a living. All I've ever done is police work. Places like the black market shops, they don't want to hire guys like me."

"Yeah," the redhead said. "Thanks. I went into law enforcement to help people, but either they hate me, or they're afraid."

"You're welcome." Kate put out her hand. All three men shook it.

She went to tell Devon, but he was snoring softly. Taking care to be quiet, she pulled up a chair and sat next to him, determined to keep watch. Fierce protectiveness burned like a beacon inside her. Now that he was finally by her side, no force on earth would ever separate them again.

She thought about the men scattered about the room. They were good men, conscientious and courageous. To be persecuted for the effects of a drug that had been forced on them was unconscionable. Surely there'd be a way to blow this thing sky-high. If they could sneak it into the media, maybe it would help undo the negative propaganda that had pushed shifters into no-man's land.

CHAPTER 14

*T*wenty-six hours later

Kate staggered as she led Devon down the hallway to her room in the underground's safe house. She'd gotten a little sleep after Devon woke, but not nearly enough. "We got lucky," she murmured.

He tightened his arm around her waist, and she leaned into him. "We sure did. We still have each other."

"That too. It was a miracle my car was in one piece. When we finally left that crappy tenement, I was expecting it to be gone, or sitting on blocks. Whoops, overshot the room." She doubled back and slapped her palm on the glass plate. The locking mechanism clicked, and she pushed it open.

Devon scooped her into his arms and carried her inside.

"Hey," she protested. "You're hurt. Put me down."

"Not that hurt." He kicked the door shut, bent his head, and kissed her, his mouth hard, demanding. She gave herself up to his probing tongue, teasing it with her own. Lust roared through her. He growled low in the back of his throat and set her down. "Cat wants out."

She understood because hers did too. Her blood heated. Everything tingled with unfulfilled need. "Shall we?"

He shook his head. "I can't. If I shift, it will rip my bandages and my stitches." He snorted. "Hell, I'd like to take a shower before I make love with you. I can smell myself, but I'm not supposed to take the bandage off for another day."

She laid a finger over his lips, beautiful, full, and sensuous. "We'll manage. Let me undress you. Then we'll go into the bathroom, and I'll give you a sponge bath."

"Is that a proposition, Miss Roman?"

"It can be anything you want." Happiness filled her. For a moment, she felt guilty. The world was falling in pieces around them, but denying themselves the pleasure of one another's bodies wouldn't change that. Ryan had told her he didn't expect to see either of them until they'd rested. She went into the bathroom and passed a hand over the left side of the sink. It began filling with hot water. She tossed a washcloth in the basin and turned to Devon who'd followed her. "You were supposed to wait in the bedroom until I got your clothes off."

"Didn't want that much real estate separating us." He closed his arms around her and pulled her roughly against him, breath hot against her hair.

She wound her arms around his back. Damn! He felt so good, so right in her arms.

He rocked his hips against her. The jut of him, hot and hard, prodded her stomach. "I can't believe how horny you make me. By rights I should be face down on the bed asleep, but all I can think about is shoving those pants down and getting inside you."

"Know what you mean." Her nipples formed hard peaks where they pressed against his chest. Her pussy turned to molten heat. She wanted to take him up on the suggestion to get her pants out of the way. He could take her standing. She'd climb up his wonderful body, settle her pussy over him, and—

Kate steadied her breathing. Her legs around him would rub

against his wound, maybe even break it open. She took a step back. "Let's do at least a cursory cleanup."

"So long as it's fast. If I wait much longer, I'll rip your clothes off and ravish you." He made a wonderful hungry cat sound. It rumbled deep in his throat.

She felt wobbly, nearly crazed with lust. He'd left his vest in the bedroom. She reached for the buttons on his shirt and undid them one by one.

Her fingers trailed down his perfect chest, starting with skin and ending on the twelve inches of bandage swathed around him. She gasped. "Christ! Must be a hell of a wound. How many stitches?" She eased his shirt off and started on his jeans.

"More than thirty. Hurt like the devil. Doc didn't use any local anesthetic. Said he'd run out."

She glanced at his feet. "Got to get your boots off. Here, lean on me." He kicked the battered, leather motorcycle boots off and pushed his pants down. They pooled on the floor; he stepped out of them.

Kate reached for his erection. She caressed it almost reverently, rubbing a drop of glistening liquid around the velvety head. "You have the most beautiful, the most perfect—" She licked dry lips.

"Hurry," her cat moaned. *"Hurry."*

Lust blazed from the depths of Devon's eyes. He batted her hands away and yanked her loose top over her head. The black watch cap came off along with her top. Bright hair spilled down her torso. His breath came fast. He bent his head and settled his mouth over a breast, sucking hard. Kate buried her hands in his hair. She slithered out of her pants, but they got tangled up in her boots, and she stumbled into him.

Devon straightened. "What?"

"Tactical error." Kate was practically beyond speech. She knelt and unlaced her boots so she could work them off. He helped her to her feet.

"You have the most incredible body." He traced a line from her shoulder to her breasts, down her stomach, and between her legs with his hand. The heat in his eyes seared her. Deep in her mind, her cat arched its back and purred its delight.

She made a grab for Devon's hand. "Five minutes," she said with mock severity. "We're grownups. We can wait that long."

He huffed. "Speak for yourself. My cock feels like it did when I was a teenager. It would get so hard, I couldn't stand it. Sometimes I'd come without doing anything to it." He grinned at her. "Sort of a look ma, no hands, orgasm."

Her hands shook with need. She wrung out the warm cloth and ran it down his body, rinsing it a few times. "There," she panted and tossed him the piece of terrycloth. "Now do me."

He pointed at the basin and snorted. "Don't you want clean water?"

Kate followed the line of his finger and laughed. "Cripes, it is pretty dingy." She pushed the button to drain the sink and started over.

She didn't care about clean water. The only thing she cared about was putting out the fire raging in her nether regions. Her body would be nicer for him if it were cleaner, though. She gritted her teeth and waited. Her clit ached with need. It was so primed, she'd come almost as soon as she finally got him inside.

He ran the warm cloth down her back, following it with his mouth. He'd already rinsed her breasts and belly. The cloth splatted on the floor, and he circled her waist with his hands. "Turn around." His voice was gravelly with passion.

She did. He sank to his knees on the bathroom's small rug and wrapped an arm around her hips. The other hand slipped between her legs, then inside her pussy. She groaned. He fastened his mouth over her clit and sucked. Fingers plumbed her. Kate tangled her fingers in his hair. Her heart pounded. The climax waiting deep inside her surged. She crushed her hips against his face and screamed his name. Her muscles closed around his fingers as she came.

He kept on sucking. His fingers pressed her G-spot. A second climax roared through her. Kate's legs shook. Once the spasms subsided, she tugged his head away from her pussy and tottered to the bed. She started to lie face down, but was afraid the temptation to shift would be too strong. She flipped onto her back, opened her legs, and beckoned.

Devon crawled up her body. He licked and kissed her starting with her toes. When he got to her breasts, she felt the head of him pressing for entrance. Her hips bucked. She had to have him inside. Now.

He let go of her nipple, supported himself on his arms, and gazed down at her. "Tell me you want me." He teased the entrance to her body, then drew back.

"I want you." She grasped his hips and tried to draw him inside, but he resisted.

"How much?" A mischievous grin lit the chiseled planes of his face. Unbound, his long hair fell over her shoulders and breasts.

"Lots." She grinned back.

"You'll have to do better than that, Roman." He moved the head of his cock in a circular motion that damn near drove her wild.

"More than I've ever wanted anyone or anything." She dug her fingers into his hips and locked her legs around him. "Please."

"Please what?"

"Please fuck me. Do it hard and fast and—" She thrashed from side to side, wild with needing to have him fill her.

Desire, feral and untamed as their cat selves, heated the air between them. She inhaled the spicy scent of their arousal. It made her even hotter. With a roar, he pushed into her, drew back, and drove himself home again.

"Yes!" She barely recognized the voice as hers. Her hips met him thrust for thrust. His teeth closed on her shoulder. The pain amped her pleasure. He swelled inside her, and got harder still. Kate's orgasm bloomed out of nowhere, catching her by surprise, and she clenched around him, holding on tight.

"Now." He growled, sounding fierce and untamed, and hotter than hell. "Now." He slammed himself into her. His cock juddered over and over. She infused all the love in the world into the places her body touched his, wanting to enhance his pleasure.

Devon collapsed on top of her.

"I love you," she murmured. "Goddamn, but I love you." Kate wanted to be more articulate, to say more, but sleep claimed her before she could even disentangle herself from his body.

Devon woke with his head on Kate's breasts and her breath warm in his hair. He rolled off her, careful not to disturb her slumber. Protectiveness rushed through him, staggering in its intensity. She was his woman, his mate. He'd make certain nothing bad ever happened to her again. He'd care for her, love her, stand by her side until death parted them.

Her eyes fluttered open. Lush lips parted in a fond smile. "Up already?"

"Just a few seconds ago. I was enjoying looking at you." He bent and kissed her forehead and her eyes, then took her in his arms. "I'm a lucky man, love."

"Oh, and why's that?"

"Because I have the most beautiful woman in the world by my side. And the smartest and most compassionate and kindest—"

"Stop, stop." She pressed her hands against his chest. "It will go to my head, and I'll become insufferable."

"I can tell you a head it has gone to." He pressed a very firm erection against her thigh.

"Mmm." She reached a hand to caress him. "I need to pee, but if you could hold that pose—"

He laughed. "Actually, I need to go too. You first." He let go of her.

Kate was just coming back from the bathroom when Devon's wrist computer buzzed. He had to follow the sound since he had no memory of where he'd taken it off. He glanced at the display and tapped a reply.

"What was that all about?" Kate eyed him. "Is our honeymoon over already?"

He snorted. "Afraid so. Ryan told us to meet him in the cafeteria in fifteen minutes."

She grinned and waggled a finger at him. "I expect a rain check on that hard-on."

Devon laughed. God but it felt good to be with Kate. "You got it, ma'am. I'm going to do a better job of cleaning up before I put my filthy clothes back on."

"I'm going to take a shower. Seems like the requisite forty-eight hours are nearly over. If you wanted to shower, it would probably be all right. Let me help you with that bandage."

He popped an antibiotic, then followed it with another. Devon wasn't certain how long they'd slept, but he'd certainly missed at least one dose. Maybe two. He quieted while Kate unwound his bandage and loosened the gauze squares.

She whistled. "Holy crap. You're lucky you weren't killed. You might've been if you hadn't been in your cat form when this happened. Mountain cats are tough."

"How'd you know I was a cat?" Devon smiled. Deep inside, his cat purred its agreement with Kate's assessment of cat virtues.

"Easy. There are hairs stuck in the wound. Text Ryan. He's a jack of all trades. I'm sure he can find you some clean clothes. Actually, tell him I need some too. I'll get the shower going."

In just over twenty minutes, he took Kate's arm, and they walked to the cafeteria. True to her prediction, Ryan had left clothes folded on the bed for them while they were in the shower. She placed her palm on the glass keypad, and the cafeteria door opened.

Max stepped forward, hand extended. Devon clasped it.

Gratitude filled him. "Thank you, sir, for believing in me. And for giving me a chance."

"You're welcome. I never do anything without ulterior motives, though. Just ask Roman."

Kate chuckled. "Glad you said it, so I don't have to bite my tongue."

Max elbowed her in the ribs. "We need your skills. Between the two of you, the entire Tracker task force has signed on to help us. Strong work." Max beamed and gestured them to a table set for four. "By the way, how's that wound in your side?"

"Better, but it will be another few days before the stitches come out. Thanks for asking, sir." Devon pulled out a chair for Kate. Once she was settled, he sat next to her.

Ryan placed covered dishes that smelled delectable on the table. "There." He glanced over his efforts with a critical eye. "Think I got everything. Does anyone need anything before I sit down? By the way, I'm Ryan." He stuck out a hand.

Devon shook it and said, "If we do, we can get it ourselves." He took a sip of wonderfully fragrant coffee. His side ached, but the discomfort was minor. He laid a hand over Kate's before tucking into ham, scrambled eggs, and toast. Surprise filled him. After he'd taken a couple of bites, he set his fork down. "This tastes like real food, not the multiple-processed crap I buy with my ration coupons."

"It is." Max munched on a square of toast. When he was done chewing, he continued. "We have farms where we raise our own food."

Devon returned to his meal. Life couldn't get much more perfect. "Do you suppose we could go by our homes and get what we can of our things?"

Max nodded. "I was going to suggest that. Ryan and some of his guys will help. Once you're done, I've enrolled both of you in a crash course in shifter police work." Max's blue gaze went from him to Kate and back. "For you—" he leveled his knife at Devon "—it will be a refresher and a bit of a heads-up how we do things. For you—" he smiled at Kate "—it will take work, but I'm sure you'll have help with your lessons."

Devon moved his chair closer to Kate and draped an arm over her shoulders. "I'll do whatever it takes to get her up to snuff, sir."

Kate leaned into him. She felt warm and wonderful pressed against his side. "I'll get back at you for this," she murmured.

"You have to catch me first."

"Enough levity." But Max smiled too. "We're on a fast track. In two weeks, we'll relocate the first of the families here. We already have the single guys on an upper level. Ryan's team is indoctrinating them now, and they'll train right along with the two of you."

He blew out a breath. "I've dropped the timeline for the nationwide push back until all of you are ready. Some of the other cities and states have Tracker elite who've defected." He slammed a fist onto the table making the dishes rattle. "We will do this right. I do not want to keep living in a world where shifters are forced to deny who they are."

Max shoved to his feet. Devon scrambled to his and stuck out a hand. "Pleasure to meet you, sir. I won't let you down."

Max gripped his hand so hard, Devon felt the bones grind together. "No, I don't think you will." He let go of Devon and clapped Kate on the shoulder. "Told you, Roman. You got a good one. Stand up. There's one more thing I need to do before I leave."

Kate got to her feet.

"Come over here next to Devon." Max drew a curved piece of dark stone from his pocket. It was about four inches long and so shiny light reflected off it.

Kate's eyes widened. "That's a ritual mating stone."

Max grinned, his blue eyes alight with pleasure. "Correct. I'm one of the twelve elected leaders of our kind, which gives me the right to conduct mating ceremonies. This one will be incomplete since I gather Devon's animal form won't be available until his stitches are out. We can get fancier later."

"Sorry to be slow on the uptake, but is this like a wedding?" Devon placed an arm around Kate's shoulders.

"Yes and no," Max said. "Weddings can be undone. This is permanent. It will bind you together forever in both your forms."

"I haven't exactly asked her to marry me yet."

Kate met his gaze and snorted. "That's the lamest proposal I've ever heard. I accept."

"You two are impossible. Hold out your right hands." Max made two quick strokes along the meaty place beneath their thumbs. "Place the cuts together until your blood mingles. Hold them there and repeat after me. *Body of my body, blood of my blood, now and forever more, I shall be yours.*"

Kate spoke the words, her amber eyes glowing with love. She'd never looked more beautiful. Devon followed. His cat did flip-flops inside him right along with his heart. Kate was really and truly his, now and forever. Joy swelled within him. He bent his head and kissed her.

Max smiled like a beneficent father. "Best part of being an elected leader," he murmured. "Wish I got to do this more often."

Devon straightened. "How would it have been different if I could've shifted?"

"This part would have been the same. Once we were done, you would have taken your animal forms and mated."

Heat rose to Devon's face. "In front of you?"

Max laughed. "Yup. Old voyeur that I am. You have a little time to get used to the idea. It will still happen, just not today." He clapped Devon on the shoulder and pulled two pieces of white cloth out of a pocket. "Here, bind your mating wounds. Save the cloths and bury them in a safe place."

"Thank you." Kate wrapped the square of linen around the base of her thumb and laid a hand on Max's arm.

"You're most welcome, Roman." He kissed her forehead. "All the best to both of you. Got to get back to Sacramento. Hovercraft's waiting." Max strode from the room.

"You guys done eating and grinning like a pair of Cheshire cats?" Ryan looked from one to the other.

"I am." Kate did a better job securing the cloth around her hand and then wrapped Devon's around his.

Devon looked longingly at the food. "Could I take the rest of this with us? I can eat en route. It'd be a shame to waste my wedding breakfast."

Ryan laughed. "Nothing like a laser wound to stir the appetite. Or a mating ritual." He piled what was left of breakfast on a plate, covered it with another, handed Devon a fork, and said, "Come on. Bring your coffees if you'd like.

"One thing I'd like you to work on," he said to Devon as he led them from the room, "is a procedures manual. If we're going to triple our ranks—and your guys will do that—we need something more standardized."

"Sure. I'd love to. I've written lots of policy and procedures manuals."

Happiness filled Devon. He took Kate's hand. No matter what the future held, the woman he loved was by his side and he had meaningful work, work that could make a difference in people's lives. There was his whole shifter side to explore and get to know better too.

His cat purred, warming him.

"You're looking pretty chipper." Kate smiled and looked even more beautiful.

"It's because I am. Thanks, love. For everything. Since we have a little time here, tell me about the twelve elected leaders. He snugged his fingers around hers.

She squeezed right back. "Well, like any other group we have a form of governance..."

~

THIS IS the end of *Roman's Gold*. The Underground Heat Series continues in *Wolf Born* where Max finds his own mate. Last book in this series is *Blood Bond*. Read on for a sample of *Wolf Born*.

ABOUT THE AUTHOR

Ann Gimpel is a USA Today bestselling author. A lifelong aficionado of the unusual, she began writing speculative fiction a few years ago. Since then her short fiction has appeared in a number of webzines and anthologies. Her longer books run the gamut from urban fantasy to paranormal romance. Once upon a time, she nurtured clients, now she nurtures dark, gritty fantasy stories that push hard against reality. When she's not writing, she's in the backcountry getting down and dirty with her camera. She's published over 50 books to date, with several more planned for 2018 and beyond. A husband, grown children, grandchildren and wolf hybrids round out her family.

Keep up with her at www.anngimpel.com or http://anngimpel.blogspot.com

If you enjoyed what you read, get in line for special offers and pre-release special reads. Sign up for Ann's newsletter on her website or her blog.

Keep reading for a teaser from *Wolf Born!*

WOLF BORN, CHAPTER ONE

Maximillian Sigayev loped up the steps two at a time as he moved from the bottom floor of the shifter underground safe house to the hovercraft port on its roof. He could have taken the elevator but he'd be cooped up in the aircraft for an hour. Any exercise was better than none. He caught himself whistling and grinned as he curved his fingers around the ritual mating stone buried deep in his pocket. It had been a pleasure to join Kate Roman and Devon Heartshorn in the traditional ceremony. He'd have to return to complete the ritual once the wound in Devon's side was completely healed, and he could shift again.

The part of the ceremony that had yet to occur was Kate and Devon's animals mating, while Max looked on to bless their union.

Max laid his palm on the glass plate next to the door that opened onto the roof. It beeped softly, and the locking mechanism released. Ever cautious, Max sent his lupine senses swirling outward to make certain no one lay in wait for him. Breath whistled from between his teeth. Up until now he'd been very lucky. His double life was bound to catch up to him.

"For God's sake, find us a mate before your penchant to take risks does us in," his wolf side growled.

"You've been pretty quiet," Max observed, not wanting to engage in a discussion about mated ones. It wasn't as if he could simply look on the vid feed or place an ad. Shifters were persona non grata. No one admitted to having more than fifty percent shifter blood—if they wanted to live.

"That's because I'm smart enough to shut up unless I have something important to say."

"We can talk once we're airborne."

"It's safe. I already checked." His wolf's tone held a supercilious edge as it frequently did.

Max trusted his wolf, but he still peered cautiously around the barely cracked door. His silver hovercraft gleamed in the morning sun. Walls rose around it on all sides to shield the safe house roof from casual eyes below. While all that brick made landing in high winds a little tricky, the added safety was worth it. Satisfied, Max strode forward, unlocked the craft's door by depressing a button on his wrist computer, and settled into the pilot's seat.

Even that quick glance at his computer showed over a hundred voice and text messages. Max growled. He hadn't been particularly forthcoming about his whereabouts when he left Sacramento the previous night. Employing a bit of shifter magic, he'd snuck away like a cat burglar. No one liked it when they couldn't find him.

He engaged the onboard generator. The craft sputtered and moved upward as soon as the electric motor developed enough torque. Getting it out of the Berkeley city airspace unobserved would be a trick-and-a-half. As California's governor, he had latitude in terms of the air quality laws, but he didn't like to flaunt his power. He set a course due east, past Hayward, to get him beyond the Bay Area corridor and over the foothills as soon as possible. Once there, he'd turn north.

He'd just settled in to review messages when his wolf snarked, *"I thought you were going to talk with me once we were underway."*

"Look." Max kept his mind-voice mild. *"I'd like to find our mated one just as much as you. We don't spend much time with shifters."*

"You always have excuses. There will be a lot more of us once everyone gets dosed with that serum."

Max pursed his lips. The wolf had a point. The intravenous infusion developed by law enforcement scientists to give cops an edge sniffing out shifters had actually pushed the ones with more than ten percent blood to full-blown shifter status. Thanks to quick thinking on Kate Roman's part, the serum was now in the underground's hands and being parceled out to strengthen and swell their ranks.

"Now you're the one who's quiet," his wolf persisted.

"Sorry. Just thinking."

"That's the problem. You think too much. Shifter partner or not, do you even remember the last time we had sex—with something other than your hand, that is?"

"Point taken. I do not want to talk about this. I have things to do."

"Finding a mate for us will never happen if you don't prioritize it." The wolf hesitated. Max hoped he was done, but he went on, *"Kate's mountain cat had to tell her Devon was her special one. She would've missed it, otherwise."* The contemptuous undercurrent was back in spades.

Max clamped his jaws together. One of the problems with these conversations was they reminded him how desperately under-fucked he was. Ever since the U.S. government had decreed shifters were to be imprisoned—or killed outright—two years before, he'd kept to himself. Before that, he'd been extremely selective, limiting his amorous escapades to other shifters since human women rarely turned him on. In his two hundred and twenty years, he'd never come across his mated one. Not that he'd looked very hard, but there weren't many candidates, either.

He grimaced. The wolf wasn't far wrong about his tendency to bury himself ass over teakettle in work. Max liked tasks where he could tweak the probability of success in his favor. Finding a mate had always seemed as unlikely as spinning flax into gold. Because he hadn't liked the odds, he'd focused his attention elsewhere.

He glanced out the hovercraft window and punched a course correction into the onboard computer system. He'd be back in the state's capitol in about half an hour. No point in antagonizing his wolf, particularly when he was probably right. *"Once we get to the other side of this war, you have my word I'll work on finding us a mate."*

The wolf subsided into snarls, apparently done with trying to convince Max of anything.

"It's not an empty promise," Max added.

"Talk is cheap."

Max snorted and bit back a laugh. *No shit.* If he had a nickel for every slick line he heard from the politicians in Sacramento, he'd be a rich man. He switched his focus to his wrist computer and attacked the message stack, texts first, then voice. By the time he landed at the hovercraft port atop his building in the state's capitol, security was waiting for him, ringed around the landing pad.

He stepped from the craft, reached in to grab his computer and briefcase, and straightened. "What?" He leveled a glance at the half dozen guards. "You're unhappy I ran off and left, and now you're going to dog me so it doesn't happen again?"

"That's about the size of it, boss." Loren, the lead security expert, sauntered forward, his lean six-foot frame encased in an immaculately pressed uniform. Dark hair was shaved close to his head. Shrewd blue eyes didn't miss much. It looked like he wanted to snap off a salute and was holding himself back.

"My office will be much too crowded with all of you in it. Once we get there, you'll need to draw straws to see who guards the door."

"You got it, boss," another guard with a blond crew cut said.

"Glad you're back," Loren offered. "It would have, ah, looked bad if something had happened and none of us even knew where you were."

Max winced at the censure in the man's voice. Loren was trying to do a job, and Max wasn't making it very easy for him. He let his gaze settle briefly on each man. "While I understand your concern, I will not be a prisoner. I appreciate that you take my safety very seriously. Believe it or not, so do I. This job is hard enough without feeling like I can't even take a crap without an audience." He pushed past the group, opened the door into the building, and walked briskly down the hall, knowing they'd follow him.

His office was at the very end of the corridor. He spoke a word so the voice-activated electronic lock would open. With one hand on the latch, he turned. "Have someone fly my hovercraft back to my house. The activation codes are in your files. Two of you at a time outside my office. No more unless there's some special public event."

He closed his door on the chorus of, *Yes, sirs* and shook his head. He'd had to pull shifter magic—and leave from his home in the middle of the night—to escape his watchdogs. With the uptick in violence, they were fiercely protective of him. Too much so for comfort.

"You could quit," the wolf commented.

Max nodded thoughtfully. *"Yeah, I could, but we need the power of this office to make sure shifters can walk free again. Between this and heading up the shifter underground, it feels like I'm living on borrowed time. These double life things have a way of imploding."*

"For once, I agree with you. What are you waiting for? Get to work."

When Max looked away from the wall screen, light was fading from the room. He'd set *Do Not Disturb* flags on every electronic account to ensure uninterrupted time to consider legislation, e-sign critical documents, and make a dent in the never-ending cavalcade of petitions from legislators. Reluctantly, he took down the flags and waited for the onslaught. It came almost immediately with a knock on the door.

"Enter."

The door flew open. Audrey, a tall, leggy, strawberry blonde with hazel eyes, charged into the room. At five-feet-ten, she was only a few inches shorter than him. As usual, her long hair was drawn into a severe bun that accentuated the exotic Slavic bone structure in her face. Her tailored black suit hugged considerable curves and exposed a lot of leg. She'd come with the job when he won the election eighteen months before and was as close to a personal assistant as he had.

Over those months, Max had expended a lot of energy not focusing on her full breasts, slender waist, and rounded rump. Today wasn't any different, and he dragged his gaze reluctantly from her perfect body.

"Sir." Barely concealed reproach danced beneath her words. "I've been waiting for you to take down your privacy curtain." She may as well have yelled at him for getting in the way of her doing her job.

"Tell me what you need." He quirked a brow, considered telling her he wasn't in the mood for her jibes, but bit back the words. She was a hell of a fine-looking woman. It always defused his ill-humor. Sexual tension simmered in the air between them, all the more palpable because he forced himself to ignore it.

"Where do you want all this?" She jiggled a large stack of documents.

He rolled his eyes. "Why are you carting paper around? Why not have someone scan them and e-send them to me? For that fact, why weren't they electronic in the first place?"

She shook her head. "These need immediate attention. They're really, really, uh, sensitive. If someone—"

"If we don't have a secure vid feed hookup here, then nowhere is safe. Dump them over there. I'll get to them tonight."

She put the stack where he'd pointed and balanced from one high-heeled foot to the other. He stared at shapely calves disappearing into stocking-clad thighs and then forced his eyes back to her face.

"Um, I was wondering if..." Her voice ran down. She started over. "See, you've been in here all day, and—"

"Whatever it is, Audrey, just spit it out. Obviously—" he gestured toward the foot high stack of reading material she'd just offloaded "—I'm far from done for the day."

Color stained her fair face. In a flash of insight, Max knew what she wanted and was sorry he'd pushed her.

"She wants sex. I smell it." The wolf chortled.

"I can't fuck her. She works for me."

"Who made that rule?"

"Is something wrong, sir?" Audrey looked at him oddly.

"Nothing at all. Why?"

"I don't know. You just got this faraway look in your eyes for a moment. It was as if part of you wasn't here anymore." The color in her face deepened. "Sorry. That didn't come out quite right. It's really none of my business."

"You never did tell me what you wanted to say." Max softened his voice. She truly was a stunning woman. Single, too, after a long, drawn-out divorce.

"Well." She studied the carpet embossed with the State Seal. "You have to eat dinner some time. I was thinking we could catch a bite and then come back, and I'll walk you through what's in those documents. I wasn't sure I should read them, but I'd already begun —" she shrugged, looking uncomfortable "—and so, I just finished them."

"Not a problem. You had to qualify for a top secret security clearance to work as my administrative assistant."

The edges of her mouth twitched into half a smile. "Funny, but it's the same thing I told myself."

"Dinner is an excellent idea." Max managed a smile. He didn't really want to take a break but saw the wisdom in an hour away from the unending flow of work. Sitting across a small, intimate table from Audrey held undeniable appeal too.

First, he needed to check on the underground. No one had messaged him for hours, and he was worried about them.

Crap! It's because I had the flags up.

Audrey had blasted through the door within seconds of him taking them down, so he hadn't had a chance to check the special scrambled feed on his wrist computer. He pushed to his feet. "Tell you what. Give me a minute to throw cold water on my face and wash up. I'll meet you at your desk."

The smile she shot him could've lit an entire city. "I'll make us reservations somewhere. Do you have a preference?"

He thought for a moment. "Sure. Call the Schenectady Steakhouse. They have sound-shielded rooms. We can bring your document pile with us and kill two birds with one stone."

Her smile faded a few lumens. "Of course, sir. I'll just gather them up—" She took a step toward the file folders.

He waved her away. "Never mind. I'll bring them with me."

Max breathed a sigh of relief when the door closed behind her. He hoped she didn't have ulterior motives, or at least, if she did, that she'd be subtle enough to keep them under wraps. He didn't want to have to tell Audrey he found her attractive, but—

"If she wants us, we should fuck her," his wolf yapped from the sidelines.

"What? You've lowered your standards. She's not a shifter."

"She has some shifter blood. I scented it."

"Yes, well so did I, but not enough to turn into anything."

"So give her some of that serum, and see what happens," the wolf suggested snidely.

"Hush. Let me see how the rest of us are doing."

Max clicked buttons on his wrist computer and scanned messages from the safe house he'd left that morning. The group of cops was assimilating well. There'd been some problems with one man's wife. She wasn't thrilled to be married to a bear, even one who promised he'd spend as much time in his human form as he could.

Kate and Devon thanked him for marrying them. He clicked a quick, *You're welcome,* still feeling warm and fuzzy from having conducted their mating ceremony. Both mountain lion shifters, they made a strong couple.

In just a few minutes, he set the computer to standby. Thank Christ there weren't any pressing issues that required his immediate attention.

He trotted to the restroom that opened off the back of his office, splashed water on his face, and rinsed his hands. Strands of hair had escaped the queue he habitually wore. Max pulled the elastic band, re-secured his shoulder-length blond hair, and tucked it beneath his suit jacket. The blue eyes that stared back at him in the mirror looked tired. He rubbed them, but it only made them more bloodshot. A quick rummage through a drawer produced eye drops.

By the time he scooped up the stack of paperwork, locked his office, and headed for Audrey's desk one floor down, he felt downright chipper. Waiting for him, bag slung over a shoulder, she held out her arms. "Here. Give me some of those."

"Nah. They're not heavy. Did you get us reservations?"

She nodded. "They weren't busy. It's only a couple of blocks. Would you like to walk?"

"Not a bad idea—" he began.

"Nope." The security officer du jour's voice rang from behind them. "We're driving you."

Max turned and raised a curious eyebrow. "Why? I was only gone for a few hours this morning. What the hell happened around here?"

The security officer blew out a tense breath. "Ever since things blew up at the Berkeley cop shop, criminals here have gone wild. Guess they're anticipating things will go south here too."

"Have they?" Max held his breath, secretly rooting for an infusion of more shifters to fight for the cause.

"Not yet, but that whole serum thing could blow up on us just like it did in Berkeley. Law enforcement here was a little behind the eight ball. Didn't start taking it until about ten days ago—"

"It's one of the things that's in all those documents," Audrey interrupted. "Once we sit down, I can fill you in."

"Okay. Let's get moving." Max met the security officer's brown gaze. "Sorry—" he eyed the man's badge, "—O'Hare. You must be new."

"Yes, sir."

"Where's the officer working with you?"

The man looked momentarily startled. "Uh, what other officer, sir?"

"Didn't Loren agree there'd be two of you at all times? I distinctly remember him acquiescing to that plan when he showed up with six of you this morning, and I felt stampeded."

"If he did, sir, no one told me. Would you like me to ring for another guard?"

Max thought about it. The extent of the security around him was ridiculous. "No. We're fine. I assume we're heading for the garage."

"That would be correct, sir."

Max gestured at Audrey to go ahead of him. They walked to the elevator, waited, and rode it down several levels toward the parking garage. Max's sensitive nose twitched. The guard smelled…odd. Fear sweat. Surely things weren't so desperate in downtown Sacramento that the man would be afraid.

Running on instincts that had rarely failed him, Max pushed the *Stop Car* button. He whirled to face O'Hare. The man's face turned white. "What are you doing, sir?"

"I'm not certain. Hand over your identification."

The guard patted his back pockets. A frantic look washed over his face, but it was gone in an instant. "Don't seem to have my wallet with me, sir. I must've left it upstairs. Maybe on your secretary's desk." He smiled weakly.

"Fine." Max pushed the button to return them to the building's next-to-the-top floor. "You can retrieve it. Audrey, text the security company. Ask them if they've ever heard of this guy."

As they neared the top floor, the odor rolling off the guard intensified: aggression mixed with fear. "I want you in front of me," Max snapped. "Now."

O'Hare—if that was really his name—lunged. Max was ready and heaved the stack of papers right at him. Audrey bit back a scream. She sounded like a hissing kettle.

O'Hare's brown eyes blazed hatred. "You're a shifter," he snarled. "Dirty, fucking traitor." He sidestepped the paper blizzard and grabbed his gun.

The elevator door opened. Audrey didn't wait for instructions. She dove through it and raced for her desk. Max judo chopped O'Hare's gun hand. The weapon clattered to the elevator's tile floor, and Max kicked it half way across the room. He engaged the button to close the elevator's door, trapping them inside. Max needed privacy. This was as good a way as any to get it.

O'Hare threw himself at Max, teeth bared. Max grappled with him and drove a knee into the man's groin. O'Hare grunted and doubled over with pain. Max linked to his supernatural shifter strength and delivered a blow to the fake security guard's neck designed to sever his spinal column. Breathing hard, he stood watch over the body until he was certain the man was dead.

It hadn't been a contest. Not really. He'd never been in any real danger. His identity was a much bigger problem than O'Hare's feeble attack. Max engaged the elevator to take him back to Audrey's level. He'd been compromised. The only question was how many people knew about him.

Christ! What the fuck do I do next?